WAR OF THE FOUR WORLDS

THE UNBELIEVABLE MR. BROWNSTONE™ BOOK EIGHTEEN

MICHAEL ANDERLE

DISRUPTIVE IMAGINATION

LMBPN Publishing
PMB 196, 2540 South Maryland Pkwy
Las Vegas, NV 89109

First US edition, April 2019
ISBN: 978-1-64202-207-0

WAR OF THE FOUR WORLDS

Special Thanks
to Mike Ross
for BBQ Consulting
Jessie Rae's BBQ - Las Vegas, NV

Thanks to the JIT Readers

Kelly O'Donnell
John Ashmore
Jeff Eaton
Peter Manis
Micky Cocker
Larry Omans
Carissa Sanford
Diane L. Smith
James Caplan
Charles Tillman
Paul Westman
Misty Roa

If I've missed anyone, please let me know!

Editor
Lynne Stiegler

To Family, Friends and
Those Who Love
to Read.
May We All Enjoy Grace
to Live the Life We Are
Called.

CHAPTER ONE

J ames stared at Thomas, his eyes narrowed. The dog stared back. Things would have been easier if the dog were acting more hostile. Even James had his weaknesses, and the dog was one of them.

It didn't matter. The animal might be stubborn, but there was no creature on Earth or Oriceran more stubborn than James Brownstone, especially when he was trying to protect someone or something he cared about.

Maybe the Vax are more stubborn than me, but God willing, I'll never meet one. And even if I do, I'll just kick their ass.

The day's contest was the latest in a long-lasting battle of wills. It was as if Thomas believed he could wear down James through sheer repetition of his demands. James didn't know if a dog could truly be so manipulative, but he'd witnessed some clever tricks from his last dog, Leeroy, enough that he wouldn't put it past this one.

Thomas barked and wagged his tail, a dastardly change in tactics.

James grunted.

That cute shit might work on Shay and Alison, but it won't work on me.

Sitting on his haunches on the immaculate tile of James' kitchen, Thomas tilted his head and let out a quiet whine, reading his master's thoughts as effectively as Whispy Doom. He padded forward and pushed his food bowl with his nose before letting out another whine.

"Dogs shouldn't have onions, boy," James rumbled, a slight frown on his face. "And there's a bunch of onions in the sauce I put in the refrigerator. It can make you sick. Why don't you understand that shit?"

Thomas barked once, his eyes flicking in the direction of the refrigerator.

James pointed toward the living room. "No barbeque sauce, even if you *are* a Brownstone. That's just the way it has to be. Now, get. Don't make me pick you up and carry you in there. That's gonna be embarrassing for both of us."

Thomas offered a final whimper and scampered off, done with his attempted manipulation of his owner and crushed by James' denial of the obviously tasty treat hidden away.

James could understand. As much as he ate barbeque, his dog must believe it was the ultimate food. And of course it was, if you were human.

A real man protected his dog as much as his dog protected him. James might have failed with Leeroy, but he would never again let a pet suffer at anyone's hands, including his own. As for others who might think hurting Brownstone's dog was a good idea, there were only so many international criminal organizations he could annihilate before there were none left.

Things had finally started to calm down, and something approaching simplicity had returned to James' existence in the last several months. There hadn't been a single level-five bounty in LA since he had taken out the remnants of the former CIA group Fortis, and Shay was content to continue planning the wedding and leave him out of the annoying process. She'd sent out some Save-The-Dates to their piles of guests with the help of the wedding planner Mary Winters.

Turns out even Shay can't handle all this complicated planning shit on her own. I'm glad she finally brought the specialist in. For a while, it looked like she was going to make me do shit.

They were still figuring out a venue, but Mary was happy to learn there was no cap on the budget for the wedding. That was one of the reasons they could send out Save-The-Dates without having a venue fully locked down even conceptually. The number of guests was irrelevant. They could always get a bigger venue, given enough money.

Huh. After the wedding and honeymoon are over, I'll have to start seriously looking into setting up my own restaurant. Probably gonna need to get some help to handle all the annoying shit on that, too. It's like everything worth doing is complicated now, even if my life has started to get simpler.

James realized after a moment that his life *hadn't* gotten simpler. He'd simply pawned off all the complicated shit to other people. Maria, Trey, and Royce were running the agency, and Shay was handling the wedding. Maybe that was how normal rich assholes got so much done in their day? He'd spent most of his life not trusting other people enough to do that, though.

And now he did. Family had changed him, or maybe it was just time.

James grunted and headed toward the living room, shaking his head. Too much self-reflection would lead to brooding, and that would just waste his time. The only things worth thinking deeply about were barbeque and his family.

His phone rang, and he pulled it out of his pocket. He frowned at the caller ID.

"Huh? Wonder why Charlyce is calling." His receptionist was volunteering at the orphanage that day. "Fuck. I hope the pipes didn't break again. If those assholes did a shitty job after Father McCartney paid them extra for the quick repair, I'm gonna go have a talk with them." James brought the phone to his ear. "What's up, Charlyce?"

"I'm sorry, Mr. Brownstone," Charlyce replied. Her voice was unsteady and had a hint of panic in it. "It's my fault. I wasn't careful enough. At least I think that's what happened. I'm so sorry."

James' mild irritation about the pipes vanished, deep concern replacing it. "What's going on? Are the kids all right?"

"Yes, yes, they're fine." Charlyce audibly swallowed over the line. "I didn't know if I should call you or Father McCartney or the police or Trey or whoever. I just didn't know. I've dealt with the rough sorts before. You can't live on the streets without doing it, but not in this sort of situation."

"What the fu…" James took a deep breath. "What's going on? Slow down and tell me."

"This nasty, nasty man came up to me as I was getting

in my car to leave. I told him to leave, or I was gonna scream so loud Jesus would come down and see what was going on. He tells me he's not gonna hurt me, but he says how he thinks we're laundering money through the orphanage, and he's been watching the orphanage and me for a few months."

James gave up and let his anger through. "What the fuck? He some cop or fed?"

"No. He said he was a *family* man." Charlyce sniffled. "He never said outright he was Mafia, Mr. Brownstone, but he did show me a gun, and he made it clear his Family doesn't like disrespect. He said if we're gonna be hiding behind kids, then we better start paying him his share, unless we want some of those kids to have some accidents. He says he knows that this is some money-laundering place for 'corporate or Hollywood assholes.' That was what he said."

James took a few deep breaths as he struggled to not crush his phone, then let out a low growl. "And what did you say back?"

"I told him the truth, Mr. Brownstone. I told him, 'You don't want to mess with this place. This isn't money-laundering. This is just a generous man.' I tried to tell him that you supported this place, but maybe that made it worse. He laughed in my face and called me foul names. He told me he didn't believe any of it, and that James Brownstone didn't need to launder money, and I was lying. I reminded him about Father McCartney, and he said he didn't care at all about no priests being involved, and he already knew about him anyway. He said this was business, and he's convinced it was some Hollywood or company thing."

"I…see." James' deep voice was laden with the promise of imminent punishment.

Fuck. I haven't been going to the orphanage lately. If that asshole had seen me there, he wouldn't have thought to even try this shit, but this stupid motherfucker is still gonna pay.

Charlyce took a deep breath. "He told me he's been watching this place for a while. Watching me. He's seen some improvements in the place, and he didn't understand how they could afford it. He told me we were going to start making weekly payments to him as a token of our respect to his Family. After all, he says they help keep the neighborhood around the orphanage safe from criminals."

A real man never fucks with dogs or orphans. Time to teach someone what a real *man is.*

"Does this piece of shit have a name?" James asked.

"Mario Dragna. Do you think they are gonna hurt the kids? Should I have called Father McCartney or the police after all? I didn't know what to do. This kind of thing never happened here before. If it was just me, I'd call the cops, but if he's watching and I try something, maybe the kids get hurt before the cops can do anything."

James grunted. "No cops. The cops will make things complicated. I'll handle this. Don't even tell Father McCartney. He doesn't need to know about this. It'll just stress him out, and within a day, this shit won't be a problem anymore, I promise you that. Mario Dragna is a very stupid asshole who is going to get a lesson in what respect really is."

"God bless you, Mr. Brownstone."

God's got nothing to do with what's about to happen.

James replied, "You did the right thing by calling me.

And don't worry about it. It's all under control now. I'll talk to you later." He hung up.

Shaking down an orphanage had to be a new low, but the Italian Mafia in LA was practically non-existent. Too much competition from different organized crime groups throughout the decades had almost chased them out of the city entirely. They had taken advantage of the chaos following the initial opening of the gates to Oriceran to re-establish a foothold, but that didn't mean they were strong. That might explain the desperate move.

There was nothing illegal about James' contributions to the place, and he was surprised the mobster hadn't done enough checking to learn that it was the orphanage the bounty hunter had grown up in. Perhaps if the mobster had, he wouldn't have made such a serious mistake.

James flexed his fingers a few times. He was itching to hit someone. Random mobsters didn't shake down places without permission. Someone might have even known exactly what they were doing and thought they could gain some leverage over him by threatening the orphanage.

I don't give a fuck what they think is going on or what their plan is. They should have known better than to threaten kids. Stupid motherfuckers. This is gonna be real fucking satisfying.

First, James needed a direct target for his wrath. He dialed Heather and waited, his heart pounding and his jaw tight. He started running through all the creative ways he could bend Mario Dragna. If the man apologized immediately, James might show him some mercy, but the local Italian Mafia still needed to clearly demonstrate that they understood the depth of their error.

"Something up?" Heather answered. "You didn't say you

would need me today. It's not a big deal, but I was going to take my son to a movie later."

"Sorry. Some shit came up."

"I almost want to say, 'It always does,' but things really have slowed down for you lately, so that wouldn't be fair. And I don't bitch because you don't mind if I do side work."

"I need an address," James replied. "I need to know who some piece-of-shit mobster named Mario Dragna works for, and I want his boss's exact address. I need to have a loud conversation tonight with Dragna's boss where we talk about respecting the Church, women, and children."

Heather whistled in appreciation. "This Dragna really, really pissed you off, didn't he? One second." The clack of her typing came over the line. "Oh, that was easier than I thought. I've got a lot of passive data collection going on in regards to the local criminal scene. Turns out I already had the info." She chuckled. "You never know when it might come in handy."

James snorted. "Yeah. So what do you got?"

"Yes, our boy Mario *does* work for the local Italian Mob. He's a new guy, from what I can tell. He was in New York, and he's only been in LA for a few months. He works as an enforcer directly under Frank Altieri. Do you know him?"

"Yeah, I know the guy. He's the local head of the Italians. I thought he was smarter than this shit. I've barely run into them, and the few mob bounties I've tracked, they understood they couldn't fucking win, so they didn't even try." James growled again. "I understand the guys fucking with Trey in Vegas, but fucking with shit here? Whatever. I don't give a shit about the reasons. Just give me his address and I'll take care of it."

Heather gave James two addresses. "The first is Altieri's mansion. The second is the restaurant he uses as his primary headquarters."

"Thanks, Heather. Keep cop drones away from both places for the next few hours. Can you do that?"

Heather laughed. "I can, but are you really going to blow up some mobster's house tonight?"

"Depends a lot on what the fucker says. I'm gonna grab some tools, and I'll think more about what I'm going to do on the way." James glanced toward the secured doorway leading to his basement.

"I better get to work. I expect overtime for this. I owe my son a movie."

"Again, sorry about that, and I'll send you a bonus. Send me a message if I need to know anything else." James ended the call.

It was time to prepare for some exercise.

James clipped a few more frag grenades to his tactical vest. He was glad that Shay was still at her archaeological symposium at the college. She might have objected to his current plan, or at least the level of pain he was planning to deliver. Although Shay understood vengeance, she had been encouraging him to dial down the general mayhem until after the wedding.

How big a point do I want to make?

James stored most of his gear in one of Shay's warehouses now, but it was always good to keep a few toys around when he didn't want to use Whispy to make his point.

He knelt by a metal case and tapped in the code before placing his thumb against the silver pad of the DNA scanner. The top of his thumb burned with the scan, and the case popped open to reveal a rocket launcher.

James considered the weapon. "Huh. That might be too much and piss off the cops." He closed the case and re-entered the lock code.

The grenades and guns would have to be enough. Besides, if he blew too many things up, it would start a big enough fire that the fire department would have to come. He didn't want them to have to clean up after his mess.

James' phone rang. He pulled it out and frowned at the caller ID.

UNKNOWN NUMBER. CALLER BLOCKED.

"Who the fuck is this?" James answered. "If you're trying to sell me shit or scam me, it's not the fucking day, asshole. If you're a politician, I'll pay you money not to run."

A man cleared his throat on the other end. "I am very sorry for your annoyance, Mr. Brownstone. I suspect it's partially my fault."

"Is this Mario-fucking-Dragna?" James growled.

"No, Mr. Brownstone. My name is Frank Altieri, and we have some things to discuss."

CHAPTER TWO

"Frank Altieri?" James rumbled. "You've got some balls calling me."

"Yeah, that I do." Altieri chuckled quietly. "I'd like to meet with you at Francesco's. It's my place. It's at—"

James interrupted with the address.

"You do your homework, Mr. Brownstone," the mob boss replied. "Not that I'm surprised."

"And why do you want to talk to me? You gonna threaten me?" James grinned at his phone, wanting the bastard to egg him on.

"Nah. I'm sorry. The problem is that I don't have certain conversations over the phone. You never know who might be listening. Even worse these days, with all this hocus-pocus bullshit. You come to Francesco's, and I'm sure it'll be worth your while."

James scoffed. "Maybe. Fine. I was planning to come anyway. At least if you're inviting me, I know you're not gonna fucking run away."

"You were planning on coming?" Altieri sighed. "Yeah, I figured. That's the problem."

"Let me make a couple of things very, very fucking clear." James' grip tightened on the phone. "I'm in a very bad mood. I'm gonna come over there to talk to you, but if this is some sort of lame-ass attempt at an ambush, you're going to fail. And after you fail, I'm going to be even more pissed. I think you know what happens when I'm pissed. Do we understand each other?"

Altieri laughed. "Yeah, you're not known for your restraint, Mr. Brownstone. I know there are a few dumb-asses out there who think they have a chance, but I pride myself on my clear understanding of my limits."

James grabbed another grenade from an open container and clipped it to his vest before closing the container, which clicked locked. "This isn't just about taking a fucking shot at me. You scratch my truck, I'm gonna be pissed, too."

"Everyone's heard about what happened to the Eyes by now. Just come over here. I think you'll be pleasantly surprised. I promise."

James grabbed one of his ugly gray coats from a rack of ten. He tried getting Shay to call them tactical coats, but she still insisted on referring to them as "ugly-ass eyesores."

"You better hope so," James replied. "Otherwise, you'll be joining the Harriken in hell."

"I understand. See you soon." Altieri hung up.

James pulled into the parking lot of Francesco's. His

ancient F-350, as well-maintained as it was, was out of place in a parking lot half-filled mostly with electric luxury and sports cars. There was a heavy concentration of Lexus and Maserati vehicles.

Compensating much, assholes?

James finished parking and stepped out of his vehicle. His long coat concealed his holster and vest. Any day he could go to sleep without having to kill people was a good one, but James wasn't always the one who made that choice. Today, the Mob was going to make it.

Altieri called me, which means this shit is even more annoying than I thought. Dragna was acting like he didn't know I was helping that orphanage, but they must have known. They're thinking I can't protect everyone and everything.

Maybe they even think they can point me at someone for them.

James' glower grew as he stomped toward the entrance. He wondered if he should bond Whispy, but decided against it. He had healing potions if he took a serious hit, and these days, with the passive regeneration Whispy did even without full bonding, the symbiont wasn't necessary for a basic low-level ass-kicking.

The tuxedoed maître d' who stood behind the dark wooden podium offered James a smile as the bounty hunter opened the tinted glass door and entered.

Most of the men filling the darkened restaurant wore nice suits. More than a few bore scars or displayed obvious bulges under their jackets like they weren't even trying to conceal the fact they were armed. Women in elegant dresses sat at many of the tables, and they cast appreciative looks James' way. The sounds of light opera filled the air—Italian, of course.

Several men glanced his way. Some looked impressed, others worried, a few angry.

James swept the dining room with a cool gaze. He couldn't start a major gunfight inside with so many non-mobsters around.

Is this Altieri's plan? Is he gonna ambush me here because he thinks I won't shoot back? I'll just go outside and wait for them to come to me.

The maître d' smiled and gestured inside. "Mr. Altieri is waiting for you in a back room, sir."

"Fine," James rumbled. "Show me."

The other man spun and maneuvered between the rows of tables, and James followed him closely. No one made any sudden movements. There were no flashes of metal out of the corner of his eye. If the mobsters were going to shoot him, it would probably be wherever he was being led. His hand twitched as he prepared to go for his gun.

The maître d' stopped in a hallway in the back in front of a door marked Private. He knocked a few times.

"Yeah?" Altieri called from inside.

"Mr. Altieri, your guest is here," the maître d' explained.

"Thanks. You go back up front."

"Yes, sir." The maître d' offered a polite nod to James before walking away.

The door opened a moment later. James' hand shot up, but he stopped before pulling out his gun. The scene in the room confused him.

A man was on his knees in front of a huge wooden

desk, his hands tied behind his back. His face was bruised and battered, and one of his eyes was swollen shut.

A tall, broad-shouldered man in a dark suit with salt-and-pepper hair stood over the man, his knuckles bloody and bruised. Frank Altieri.

Another mobster stood beside the door, his expression blank, no weapon in his hands. James doubted the mobsters were going to try to win against him in hand-to-hand. Everyone had seen enough videos of him kicking people into walls to know why that was beyond a terrible idea.

James stepped inside, and the closest mobster closed the door behind him before crossing his arms and leaning against the wall.

Altieri grabbed the kneeling man's hair and yanked his head up. "Do you got something to say, Mario?" He pointed to James. "To that man who went to all the trouble of coming over here and took time out of his busy day?"

"I-I'm sorry," Mario sputtered out, blood dripping from his mouth.

James frowned. "What the fuck is going on here?"

Altieri released Mario, and the man slumped forward. "I'm sorry for making you come down here, Mr. Brownstone, but I couldn't talk about any shit the feds might overhear. At least here, we can talk in private. Even got some nice anti-magic shit set up." He gestured toward Mario. "I want to make something clear. Mario was not authorized for the money-making opportunity he pursued. Even *if* that orphanage wasn't associated with you, that shit's not allowed."

James grunted and nodded, confusion still weighing on

his mind. He'd been so convinced it had been a high-level mob plot against him that hearing the opposite left him confused and a little unmoored. A man didn't grab a half-dozen grenades and just *not* use them.

"So, what…random guys working for your crew just go and fuck orphanages up?" James asked.

Altieri clucked his tongue and peered down at Mario with a mixture of contempt and irritation. "Here's the thing: I do encourage the guys to show, you know, *initiative* in terms of their revenue collection skills. Mario here, he's new. He came from a different…organization. I don't think he realized how things work out here." The mobster gestured with his hands. "First of all, I'm a man who still goes to Church, so I would never allow someone to mess with a Church-run orphanage. Second, I don't believe in screwing with kids. That's just a personal thing. It's what separates us from savages."

James narrowed his eyes. "According to my witness, your guy Mario here seemed convinced there was some sort of money-laundering going on."

"Yeah, that's what I've heard, and as I explained to Mario, that doesn't mean shit in terms of how we deal with kids and Church orphanages." Altieri shook out his bruised hand. "That's the real problem here—sloppy employees. I'll admit it reflects poorly on my leadership."

James grunted. "That reminds me, the woman your man insulted wasn't just some volunteer. She's one of my employees."

Altieri laughed and shook his head. "Mario, you complete and utter fucking dumbshit. No wonder you had to leave New York." He looked at the other silent mobster in the room. "What am I always saying about opportunities?"

The other man snorted. "Do your due diligence."

"That's right." Altieri clucked his tongue again. "Due diligence saves us from shit like James Brownstone coming at us because..." He stomped toward Mario, his eyes blazing with rage. "...some piece of shit threatened his orphanage and disrespected his employee!" he screamed.

James frowned. He almost felt a little bad for Mario at this point.

Altieri took a step back and adjusted his tie, his slight smile and calm expression returning. "I'm assuming that since you came in that less-than-fashionable long coat, you're probably packing, right, Brownstone?"

"I wouldn't walk into a mob restaurant unarmed. That's just stupid."

"Not that you need that shit. I know all about your magic armor. I've seen video of it." Altieri pointed at Mario. "I understand respect, Mr. Brownstone. We Family men live and die by it, and Mario has disrespected you and yours. So I offer his life to you."

James glanced at them. Ironically, he'd been prepared to gun down a dozen people, but the idea of killing some poor bastard who was already half-beaten to death whimpering on the floor held no appeal.

James shook his head. "Just put him on a plane out of town. If he ends up dead here, it'll probably cause trouble for both of us in the long run. The main reason I came here was to protect the orphanage." He glowered at Mario. "But don't ever even *think* about coming back to LA."

Mario nodded quickly.

Altieri nodded at the other mobster. "Take his ass out back. Get him some tickets, and put him in a Currus out of state. I hear Maine's pretty this time of year."

The thug opened the door, marched to the cringing Mario, and yanked him up by his collar. He shoved the thug through the door and closed it behind them.

Altieri sucked in a breath and took a seat behind his desk. "You run a business. You ever have any trouble with problem employees?"

"A few." James shrugged. "I've got a retired Marine who whips them into shape."

"I should get me one of those." Altieri flexed his bruised hand a few times. "I still feel bad about this, so I want to make further amends. You don't want blood. That's fine. You're right. Fucking feds are always up my ass, and bodies lead to trouble." He frowned. "No one has any respect anymore. My grandpa used to talk about the old days. Being a Family man meant something back then. Now everyone's just a half-assed thug in a suit."

James grunted. "I don't really want anything from you. I don't need mob favors."

"Sure, sure. I get that you're the Granite Ghost, and you've got to maintain a certain distance from me and mine." Altieri snapped his fingers. "But it's the orphanage that was threatened, not you directly, so maybe I'll make a donation to the orphanage."

James shook his head. "Father McCartney won't accept blood money. It took him a long time to even accept *my* donations because they were from bounty hunting."

"I could do something indirectly."

James' mouth twitched. "Are you trying to do what Mario thought was going on? Don't."

Altieri waved his hands placatingly. "Whoa, calm down there, Mr. Brownstone. I'm not trying to do anything. No one's attempting to manipulate you. I heard you walked right up to some asshole who could control people's minds and still put his ass down." He laughed. "To be honest, I'm not sure how much longer we can even run a true underground business in this town with you and your boys and girls breathing down our necks. I've even been thinking about going legit."

"I don't give a shit. Keep your guys from having bounties, and you won't have to deal with my people or me. You care so much, then donate to some other charity that helps orphans." James turned around and headed toward the door. He stopped when his hand touched the handle and looked over his shoulder. "I've got something you can do if you really feel bad."

"Sure, anything."

"I want to invite you and your top guys to our wedding. Pick like the top eight or something." James shrugged. "I don't give a shit about your organization, so I don't care. Just make sure you're there too."

"What?" A mask of confusion took over Altieri's face. "Your wedding?"

"Yeah, it's gonna be the last day of July. I'd give you a Save-the-Date, but I didn't bring any with me. Sorry. If you call the agency and ask, they'll be able to give you the information and make sure you're on my guest list. We don't have the venue selected yet, but I'll make sure full transportation is provided if it isn't somewhere you can get to easily."

Altieri blinked a few times and tilted his head as he processed the odd turn in the conversation. "You want me and my top eight guys at your wedding? Which, from the sound of it, is going to be in some weird out-of-the-way place?"

James nodded and grinned. "It would show respect." His grin vanished. "And not coming after I invited you would be disrespectful."

"You got, like a registry, or some shit like that?" Altieri asked, his voice unsteady. "I don't really know what to buy you as a gift."

"Shay and I don't need shit. We just want people there. And to be clear, I also don't want any bullshit happening in LA on my wedding day, even if I'm not here."

"Bullshit?" Altieri asked.

James grunted. "Yeah. Bullshit. I'm gonna invite all the top underworld people, and they're gonna make sure that the day doesn't end with trouble that's gonna give the cops a headache. When the cops get a headache, *I* get a headache, and I don't want to go on my honeymoon and come back to some mob war shit, understood?"

Altieri replied with a shallow nod.

James opened the door. "Good. See you in July. Don't worry, I'll make sure you get a formal invitation. Everyone likes weddings, right?"

"Yeah." Altieri swallowed, as pale as if he had just been sentenced to death. "Everyone likes weddings."

CHAPTER THREE

Trey sighed and leaned back on his grandmother's couch. The damned thing was older than he was. Hell, it had a good ten years on him. He kept offering to buy her new furniture, but she refused him every time.

"Nana, I don't need you in there getting me anything. I'm a grown man. I can get my own lemonade."

The elderly woman snorted from the kitchen, her expression hidden by the wall. "Boy, just because you all fancy now with your magic gloves and suits don't mean I can't take care of you. Let your nana feel useful."

It's taking her even longer than normal.

Trey waited a painfully long time as his grandmother crept around the corner, a glass of lemonade in one hand and a supporting cane in the other. He accepted the glass and let out a sigh of relief once she finally sank into in her recliner and the risk of a fall vanished.

"I heard that, boy," Nana Garfield muttered. "You think I'm old and useless. I know you're thinking it every time you come back to town these days. You done went off to Las Vegas, and you've let all that glitz and glamour impress you, even though you're from LA."

Trey shook his head. "I don't think you're useless, Nana, but I *do* think you've spent a lifetime looking after worthless ingrates like me, and it's time for you to take a rest." He smiled softly. "And I worry about you. Did you think Auntie Charlyce wouldn't tell me about the fall? I'm a bounty hunter. I sniff out secrets and lies for a living."

Nana Garfield scoffed. "That woman—she's making such a big deal of it. She lived on the streets and she's seen a lot worse, and she's acting like I'm going to die just because I took a little fall. People fall all the time. What of it?"

"You're lucky she was here, and you're lucky you didn't break anything. You don't always have your phone next to you. If you hurt yourself and no one's here, what are you going to do then, huh? Even at the agency, we rarely do a job alone for that reason. It wouldn't be so bad if you at least used a smart speaker or something."

Nana Garfield frowned. "I don't need no robot spy in my living room. I don't trust no robots, I can tell you that. Humans and Oricerans, they are all parts of God's creation. Robots are made by people and we're sinful and fallen, which means what we've created is dangerous when it's not about praising the Lord."

Trey groaned and took a deep breath before responding. Yelling at his grandmother wouldn't accomplish anything. "Nana, I just don't want you breaking your hip and lying there in pain, especially since Auntie Charlyce and I don't live with you no more. She also told me, by the way, that she asked to move back in and you told her no. What are you thinking? That would solve everything."

"I'm thinking that girl finally got off the Devil's drugs and is working a normal, honest job. She deserves to have a life, not be looking after me." Nana Garfield shook her head. "I won't do that to her. No, I won't."

"Okay, I hear that. What about moving in with me? You'd like Las Vegas. It's not all casinos and clubs, you know. Plenty of elderly folks like it."

"Las Vegas is nothing but sin, and that takes some effort, considering I live in LA. Not only that, I'm not gonna inflict myself on you. Don't you get it, boy?" Nana Garfield frowned.

"It's not like that." Trey sighed. "You're not a burden. You deserve it. I could get a bigger place. I'm sure Zoe won't mind."

"No. I won't be doing that." Nana Garfield leaned back in her chair and let out a long, labored breath. "You and Charlyce have both made me proud. I'm not ready to meet the Lord yet, but I when I do, I know I can go with fewer regrets since some of my children and grandchildren have escaped from the pain and poverty that I worried y'all would be stuck in. That same pain and poverty I couldn't help free you from. It's your time now, and I want to give it to you. You don't need to be looking after some old woman."

Trey stood. He didn't want to raise his voice to his grandmother, but the woman's intransigence was more frustrating than a level-one bounty who refused to accept that he was outclassed.

From what Charlyce had told Trey, she had come by to

visit, only to find the older woman moaning on the floor. Charlyce had called an ambulance, and the ER doctor had said it was a miracle Trey's grandmother hadn't shattered her hip.

Trey had the resources, monetary and magical, to protect and save his grandmother if he were around, but he wasn't around anymore. Not enough, anyway. He was hours away in a different city, not able to drop everything at a moment's notice and drive to her house.

"Charlyce also told me you haven't been taking all of your pills," Trey noted.

"Pills, pills, pills. I take pills to take care of the problems caused by the other pills." Nana Garfield shook her head. "Sometimes I forget, but it ain't the end of the world. I'm still here."

Trey looked down at the floor. His next best plan would require her cooperation, and he had his doubts. He forced a look of confidence onto his face and lifted his head. "If you won't move in with Charlyce or me, and you won't let Charlyce move back, maybe we should consider other options."

"What other options?" Suspicion colored Nana Garfield's face.

"You know…like a place where older folks gather together but still have some independence."

"I ain't living in no home." Nana Garfield glared at him. "You ain't sticking me in one. You better bring Mr. Brownstone and every bounty hunter in your agency if you try to force me into one, because I'm gonna fight with every last ounce of my strength." She lifted her cane and shook it menacingly.

Trey groaned. "No homes. I get it. It's like I said, a place where you can have some independence, like an assisted-living apartment. You would still have your own place, but there are more people around your own age, and you have people checking in on you."

"I ain't need that." Nana Garfield shook her cane at him again. "I've got all the ladies at church. Plenty of friends. Why leave behind my nice house for new friends when I've already got them?"

"This house is too much for one old woman to keep up, and you know it."

"I'm the one who has to live in it, boy. You mind your own place and don't worry about mine." Some of the anger faded from Nana Garfield's eyes. "Besides…"

Trey's brow furrowed. "Besides?"

Nana Garfield released her cane and pointed to the framed pictures filling a glass cabinet in the corner. "Memories, good and bad—that's what this place is. I get that for you, Trey, this place is probably what you think of when you think of your old life of pain, but it's not like that for me." She sighed. "I'm old, and my time is coming sooner rather than later, but I want to spend my final years with all my memories, not in some strange apartment with a bunch of people I don't know." She gestured to the front window. "It makes even less sense now to leave. Because of all you boys getting honest, good-paying jobs and Mr. Brownstone, the neighborhood's changing. Businesses are coming back. Other young people can get jobs, and jobs bring hope for the future, where there was so little hope here before."

She smiled. "I don't want to leave now, when everything's changing. When the entire neighborhood is coming back to life. No, I want to die in this house. Not anytime soon, Lord willing, but when I do pass, I want it to be here, or in church. That's fine, too. It will cut the time for my trip to Heaven."

Trey laughed. "You're too stubborn for me to win against, Nana."

"Promise me, Trey. Promise me you won't try to make me leave."

"Fine, I won't." Trey put up a hand. "But you can't keep pretending you've got everything under control. If you don't want to move, and you don't want to let family in, then let me pay for a cleaner to come maybe a few times a week and a nurse to check on you a few times a week."

Nana Garfield frowned. "I ain't sure about having strange folks visiting my house, but if that is what it takes to get you to agree, then I'll do it."

"Good." Trey slapped his hand over his breast pocket of his expensive black suit. "Remember, Nana. I'm rich now. I've got tons of money, so let me share it with you. Every time I take down one of those level threes or fours, even after the agency cut, it's a huge amount of money." He leaned forward, eagerness on his face. "You're right. The big man gave the boys and me an opportunity and almost all of us took it, so now we're in a much better place. I know I am, so I can do what I could never before: make sure that my family is taken care of." He grinned. "I'll hire all the sweet-ass male nurses you need. Anything to keep you in the home."

"Oh, I don't need some hunky man checking in on me."

Nana Garfield considered that for a moment. "But it wouldn't hurt none, either."

CHAPTER FOUR

"A trip to Earth?" Calal asked, his blond eyebrows raised. "I don't see why you want to go there. It's very unpleasant, I've heard, and also from what I've heard, the magic is still minimal. It needs a few hundred years to become comfortable, I'd say." The Light Elf gave his friend a look of disgust, unsure why he would want to do so something so foolish.

A cool wind blew over them. Both elves stood in a guard tower at the edge of a high plateau overlooking a modest trade town in an otherwise unremarkable area of Oriceran. Stone and wood buildings were interspersed with the occasional ostentatious metal or crystal tower, but the town was too far from any of the mines in the region to have a major concentration of wealth.

The other Light Elf, Mear, shrugged. "It'd be more interesting than being a guard in a town where nothing ever happens. The most exciting thing we've done in the last year was break up that brawl with all those drunken dwarves from that mining caravan. This isn't why I spent all that time training. This was supposed to be an opportunity, but it feels more like a punishment."

Calal laughed. "I think that's a good thing. What do you want, the Great War?" He shuddered. "Random battles against rogue witches, Atlanteans, and Mountain Striders? Peace is underappreciated."

"No, I'm not saying that. I'm just saying that something other than an arrogant gnome or thieving pixie would be nice now and again." Mear scoffed. "A visit to Earth would at least be interesting. Different. I've talked to several people who have gone, and they've enjoyed it. The stores are fascinating compared to ours."

Calal shrugged, disbelief still written on his face. "Travel more around Oriceran if you're so bored. There's far more to see here than you'll find on Earth. Most of their magical races still hide from the rest of the planet. The humans infest it like a cancer, and there are so many of them."

Mear chuckled. "That seems interesting. Those teeming cities must be a sight, indeed. Still, I'd like half a chance to prove myself."

"All the recent trouble dates back a few decades, but things aren't too bad, and I think that's perfect. Rhazdon's been handled, and the gates are stable, though opening. I was half-afraid the non-magical humans would start pouring over here and bringing all their noxious technology with them, but you barely see them except in the larger cities." Calal gestured to a convoy of beaked men riding giant, colorful lizards. "They're a long way from home, aren't they? I'm surprised to see desert folk out here."

"I suppose," Mear answered, his gaze distant. After a moment, he pulled out a gleaming long sword. "This sword is thousands of years old. The magic on it helped one of my ancestors end a Drow rebellion, but what I am doing with it? Nothing. Threatening drunkards into submission." He scoffed. "I knew I should have gotten a position as a royal guard when I had the chance a hundred years back. At least I could have been involved in the murder investigation. That would have been interesting."

"Not really." Calal marched to the edge of the tower, watching the caravan proceed farther into the town. "They kept it tightly contained and closed, and they brought in… Well, it turns out she wasn't just a human, but they didn't know that at the time. They were trying their best to keep many things secret."

The air thickened, and Calal's hair stood up on the back of his neck. A strange sensation passed through him. His first instinct was to call it magic, but it didn't feel like any magic he'd ever sensed before in the two centuries of his life.

"Did you feel that?" he asked quietly.

Mear nodded and pointed. "That felt like it came from farther down." He leapt out of the tower. A quick wind spell allowed him to fall halfway down the steep slope and land as if he'd taken a single step. Calal joined him a moment later.

They were now on the outskirts of the town, on the opposite side from the desert folks' caravan. A few small warehouses lined the marble streets. A smattering of elves and a few other races stood along the street, gesturing and talking to themselves, confused and concerned looks on their faces.

The strange pulsing energy lingered.

"We're obviously not the only ones who sense it," Mear murmured. He summoned a quick shield. "I've heard rumors that now that the Drow don't have a queen, they might try to return to a life of conquest. Attacking a border town would be a good place to test their strength."

Calal scoffed. "I've heard just the opposite. Besides, this doesn't feel like Drow magic." Despite his disbelief, his heart pounded, and he also cast a shield spell. Sparkling energy surrounded him.

"Who then? More Rhazdon adherents?"

"It's probably just someone opening a huge portal or another gnome prank."

An opaque dark hole appeared in the air ten feet above the ground, and lines of dark green energy crackled across the portal.

"See?" Calal pointed. "Just because something's a little different, doesn't make it dangerous. We'll inform the new arrival about proper protocol once they're through, though."

A two-armed, two-legged humanoid figure emerged from the portal and dropped to the ground, landing on its feet with a thud.

Calal didn't recognize the species. He wasn't sure if the mottled silver-green metallic outer layer surrounding the creature was its natural skin or some type of armor. Two sharp blades made of the same material extended from the tops of both arms, and although it had a head, the creature lacked any obvious eyes or other distinguishing facial features. Two curled razor-tipped segmented appendages extended out of its shoulders, twitching. They looked as if they could reach farther than the creature's arms if fully extended.

Calal sighed. From the look of it, the creature probably was some underground race. Maybe a Halican relative or something of that nature. That would explain its appearance and the odd sensation associated with its portal.

Mear stepped forward. The music of a quick Light Elf translation spell followed, although they could be tricky with non-flesh-based races. "May we help you? I'm afraid I don't recognize your race." He looked at Calal, who shrugged back, as clueless as his friend. "This is the town of Alazi."

The new arrival stared at Mear for a moment, not moving. Then a sudden loud roar had Mear jumping back, his hand on the hilt of his sword.

"We are the Vax," the new arrival declared, the translation spell working after all. The deep, foreboding tenor of the original voice remained, unaffected by the spell. "We are the Purifier. Your planet represents a threat. This ends your warning. You will die." The Purifier slowly raised an arm.

Calal jerked up his hand and made a few quick movements. Melodious notes flowed into an alarm spell to summon additional guards. He followed with a remote transmission spell, his heart racing. Mear had gotten his wish. The latest threat appeared far more dangerous than a drunken dwarf.

"Vax?" Mear murmured. "I know that name, but from where? And what do you mean, you are the Purifier?" He pointed his sword at the Vax. "No matter. You will stand down immediately and surrender. Your threats risk inflaming public unrest. I don't know if you're a criminal or if this is a bizarre act of war, but the Great Treaty is in force, and we were hired to protect this town in any event."

The Purifier took a single step toward Mear, and the elf raised his free hand and murmured an incantation. Strands of rope appeared and wrapped themselves around the arms and legs of the Purifier. The elf smirked, confident of his victory.

The Vax ripped through the ropes with ease and let out a long, low growl.

"If you don't stand down, we'll be forced to harm you," Calal explained. "Please don't force us to do that."

The Purifier stopped. He turned his head slightly, but it was hard to know what he was looking at given the lack of eyes. A green bolt blasted from his right blade and struck Mear.

The elf flew backward, hissing in pain. He landed on his back, his sword in his hand. His shield failed, but given the burn on his chest, the magic had saved his life.

The people who had come to see what was happening shouted in alarm, scattering.

Calal pointed his sword and rattled off an incantation. A ring of fireballs appeared and exploded against the Purifier, producing nothing more than minor scorches. A creature immune to fire was a dangerous beast indeed.

Mear leapt to his feet and strengthened his shield. A bright red aura gripped his sword, and he charged the enemy. He swung for the shoulder. He shouted in triumph when the enchanted blade sliced through the creature's arm and separated it from his body.

The silver-green metallic limb fell to the ground, and the Purifier howled in pain and anger.

Mear stepped back with a cocky grin on his face. "Such threats, but you're not so powerful, are you, Vax? I can take you apart piece by piece." He brought his blade back. "You're not worth such an ancient blade, but so be it."

Calal's gaze dipped to the severed limb. He could make out the bloodied back of a red-skinned arm. The Purifier was an armored creature, not some ground-dwelling race of metal and stone.

Silver-green metallic tendrils shot from the Purifier's wound, twisting around each other and forming the outline of a new limb.

"It's not over," Calal shouted.

Mear placed a hand behind him, and an air burst spell launched him forward. He raised his sword for a decapitation strike, but his blade met the neck of the beast with a loud, reverberating clang.

The elf's eyes widened in surprise, and only his tight grip around the hilt of the blade kept it from flying away as he jerked to a sudden stop. He jumped back, gritting his teeth. There was only a shallow cut in the neck.

"Mear, be careful!" Calal shouted. He took his opportunity to fire a few bolts of light magic. The first made the Purifier stagger back with a shallow blackened hole in his armor. The second barely marred him. Silver-green metallic tendrils filled the hole, and the Purifier's arm continued to regenerate.

Mear backed up, shaking his head. "Protected your

head, did you? Cleverer than I gave you credit for." He swung again, this time going for the other arm, but his blade bounced right off, leaving only the barest hint of a scratch. He tried a third attack, but this time the Vax met Mear with his own blade.

The Purifier's weapon sliced through Mear's enchanted long sword and the top half clattered to the marble stones of the road. Both pieces stopped glowing.

"Impossible," Mear shouted, still gripping the hilt. He spun in time to avoid the Vax's blade taking his head off, but one of the razor-tipped shoulder appendages shot forward and speared him through the chest. He coughed up blood, blinking down at his wound in surprise. The shimmer of his shield vanished, and his head lolled forward.

"No!" Calal shouted. He launched more light bolts, but they did nothing.

The Purifier brought Mear's body closer and pushed him off the bloodied appendage with his armored foot.

A green bolt erupted from the tip of the other appendage and slammed into Calal's shoulder. Pain exploded through his body as he fell to the ground. Unlike the first attack on Mear, Calal's shield had done nothing. A huge blackened hole surrounded by charred flesh ran through his shoulder.

In the distance, several other guardsmen were approaching, some zooming along on slabs of earth, others soaring through the air with the help of magic.

Flashes of green light danced across the remaining arm blade of the Purifier. The first arm was halfway regenerated. The appendages swung back and forth, blasting green hellfire into buildings, fleeing people, and animals. Two gnomes emerged from a nearby building and summoned a huge wall of ice in front of the Purifier.

A moment later, bright green beams blasted from the arm blades and carved through the wall, buildings, and anyone unfortunate enough to be in the way, including some of the newly arriving guardsmen and the gnomes. The top of the ice wall fell back, smashing into the ground and sending up a shower of ice shards and dust.

Calal fought unconsciousness as pain suffused his body and gripped his shoulder, murmuring a healing spell. The Purifier wasn't the only one who could regenerate.

Lightning crashed into the monster, then acid. The surviving guardsmen were counterattacking.

Some of the attacks did nothing, but others forced the monster back and wounded it, only for its regeneration to continue. Always, the next similar attack accomplishing nothing.

Roaring, and with his arm regenerated, the Purifier swept the area with twin beams of death. His appendages continued their staccato spitting of the green bolts. They burned deep into any unprotected Oriceran they encountered.

The roof of a nearby building collapsed, and several people inside screamed as the heavy stone crushed them.

Calal staggered to his feet, not bothering with his sword. He shoved his hands forward and began chanting a complicated paralysis spell. They didn't need to kill the Purifier. If they could disable him, they could get more reinforcements and figure out some way to handle the creature. All beings had a weakness.

The Purifier's back was turned to the elf as the creature mowed down the newest guardsmen arrivals, their defenses not protecting them from his beams.

Bodies littered the ground, and smoke poured from the burning buildings.

Calal finished the spell, and a glowing glyph appeared on the back of the Purifier.

"That should hold you, monster," Calal spat.

The glyph disappeared, and the monster let out a growl. He advanced, and this time massive lines of juddering energy appeared on his blades. The Purifier's shoulder appendages stopped firing, and the tips grew brighter.

Calal swallowed. "Can nothing stop you?" He hurled an ice lance, a fireball, and blasts of pure light magic at the Purifier. Each spell landed, but the creature didn't seem to notice or care.

The green light grew blinding, and Calal shielded his eyes.

A massive green blast exploded from the Purifier and smashed into a nearby crystal tower, obliterating the structure and some of the smaller wooden buildings nearby. The shockwave knocked Calal flat on his back.

The elf groaned and craned his neck up. A massive cloud of crystal shards spread across the sky and rained down in the following moments.

Calal sat up in time for the Purifier's next major attack, which blew away several smaller buildings in one blast. Not a single undamaged building remained standing in the area. He didn't bother to survey the bodies.

Somehow cruel fate had left him alive against an unstoppable monster. He stared, his breathing shallow, his mind refusing to offer any useful tactics. He did nothing as Vax beams and blasts ravaged the area.

The Purifier advanced toward the town. All the carnage and destruction so far had been limited to the edge.

Calal fell to his knees and began chanting a new spell. If he couldn't stop the Purifier, he had to save everyone.

The Purifier halted his advance and slowly turned around. The elf continued casting his spell as the monster raised his arms and charged a beam attack.

Magic filled the air. As Calal spoke, his amplified voice shouted from above, as if a god were speaking to the town. "Flee! Run! Evacuate! The smoke isn't a normal fire. An unknown monster immune to magical attacks has slain the guard. You can't win against this monster, regardless of your power."

The last thing Calal saw was the bright green blast of the Purifier's beam before it incinerated him.

CHAPTER FIVE

Senator Johnston settled into the comfortable high-backed chair at the long table. The President and Vice-President were absent, but the National Security Advisor and the Chairman of the Joint Chiefs of Staff weren't.

He wasn't sure what was going on, only that he'd been ordered to come to the White House for a matter of "significant interplanetary concern." The newest Oriceran Ambassador to the United States, an elegant female elf with dark hair named Yona, sat near the front of the table, her lips pursed and anger all but visibly radiating off her.

Senator Johnston felt bad for the woman. She'd only been on the job for a few months, and the complexities of Earth-Oriceran relations would make any being faint from stress. Even if they had been watching—and in some cases manipulating—humans for millennia, Oricerans didn't always understand them.

It was rare that Senator Johnston was not clear what was going on, and the presence of Ambassador Yona suggested the issue wasn't focused on non-Oriceran aliens. Between the Alliance and Fortis, things had gotten unnecessarily complicated in the last year. He preferred it when the CIA and a few other black ops groups were grabbing the spare alien or artifact.

The National Security Advisor cleared his throat as a few more officials filtered into the room. "Thank you for joining us. We'd like to get started. I'll skip the bullshit and make it clear what made us call this meeting." He nodded at the elf. "Ambassador Yona contacted us to let us know there was a brutal assault yesterday on a small town on Oriceran. The single perpetrator laid waste to the town and murdered hundreds of people despite the presence of trained Light Elf guards. The Light Elves have reason at this time to believe the culprit was not of Oriceran origin, and may have launched his attack from a base in the United States. If that's the case, we'll have to treat this as a major terrorist incident and do our best to aid the Oriceran authorities in the apprehension and/or elimination of this terrorist."

Everyone at the table tensed. Even though the nations of Earth weren't formal signatories to the Oriceran Great Treaty, most, including the US, had signed various other treaties. A massive attack like the one just described could easily push Oriceran into war against an Earth nation, a situation that no one on either side wanted. Senator Johnston knew what the US would do if some fresh-out-of-the-portal Oriceran strolled into a random town and slaughtered hundreds of people.

Ambassador Yona raised her hand, and musical notes filled the air. A moment later a shimmering image appeared, the point of view of someone confronting a figure in chillingly familiar biomechanical armor. "These are the last moments of one of the Light Elf guards killed in the town of Alazi. The elf's name was Calal."

"Vax?" came a voice from the image. "I know that name, but from where?"

———

The magical footage ended with the death of Calal.

Ambassador Yona waved her hand, and the image disappeared. "This evidence is clear. There's only one being who uses such armor. We've tracked the activities of James Brownstone in the past. We know he traveled to Oriceran and engaged in a battle with the Drow Queen, but because the Drow didn't lodge a complaint, we let that slide. This is beyond unacceptable, however."

Her hands curled into fists. "We don't care what you think of this man or how useful he is, we will not allow him to slaughter entire towns. If you attempt to shield him, it will be a violation of existing treaties and a potential act of war. We demand justice, and we will seek it." She slammed a fist on the table. "His level of danger far exceeds even sending him to Trevilsom, and we intend to bring together a group to hunt him and send him to the World in Between."

"And where is the killer now?" Senator Johnston asked.

"After the destruction of the town, the murderer continued marching in a southwesterly direction. Currently, we're watching him from afar while we evaluate our options. It's unclear to us what his destination or goal is, since he's come close to another town and several villages but hasn't attacked them."

When the magical movie had begun, Senator Johnston's heart had started pounding so much he thought he was going to have a heart attack right there in the conference room, but as the carnage unfolded, calm resignation set in.

The politician had two problems to handle, most likely soon to be three, but at least one of them he could handle immediately without much effort. He still would have to tread lightly, because even though he had been in politics for decades, the woman sitting across the table from him was likely older than the United States.

"If James Brownstone killed a bunch of Oricerans, and if we were shielding him," Senator Johnston began, "then everything you said would be true, and we would offer our full cooperation. But that creature isn't James Brownstone."

Ambassador Yona scoffed. "If it's not him, then who is it? You saw through the eyes of a man there, and you heard that it was a Vax."

Senator Johnston summoned his best magic: a disarming smile. "You mentioned tracking James Brownstone, but I doubt you track him like we do. You said this attack was yesterday, and you said he's still on Oriceran?"

"Yes. So? What of it?"

"James Brownstone is currently in Los Angeles, and he hasn't left Los Angeles for several weeks. We could go visit him right now if you wanted. He's at home."

Uncertainty passed over the ambassador's face. "What are you saying?"

Senator Johnston let out a long sigh and glanced at the

National Security Advisor and the Chairman of the Joint Chiefs of Staff. "I'm saying we've got a different nightmare scenario. I'm saying that one of Brownstone's people, a Vax, has finally shown up. One of the boogeymen of the galaxy is now on Oriceran, and from the show he just put on, apparently being tough doesn't just apply to James Brownstone."

The faces of half the people in the room tightened. Some of them swallowed.

Ah, you all were hoping, weren't you? Hoping it was Brownstone, and we could just agree to drop a nuke on him.

The National Security Advisor turned to Ambassador Yona. "The US government is willing to commit assets to aid in defense of Oriceran against this hostile extra-terrestrial threat."

"Assets?" the elf replied. "What assets? We've already sent a second group after him who used even more powerful magic than the first time, and they barely hurt him before being killed. You saw what happened as well. A limb shorn, and regenerated a short while later."

"We don't know how our aircraft will perform on Oriceran," the Chairman of the Joint Chiefs explained. "But I'm willing to bet that bastard might not bounce back so easily if we dropped a few JDAMs on him."

Ambassador Yona frowned, not understanding the military jargon.

"Lots of bombs, basically," Senator Johnston explained. "But unfortunately, General, I actually doubt that would work."

The other man looked at him with a frown. "You do?"

Senator Johnston nodded. "Everything we know about

these Vax suggests they adapt quickly to attack types. James Brownstone was a child when he came to Earth. It might very well be that the older Vax have a stronger baseline of defense. After all, it'd be foolish to send out your soldiers to worlds with advanced technology if all it took was one good bomb hit. I think we have to assume at this point that all non-nuclear conventional weapons will be ineffective against an armored Vax."

"You're suggesting this new arrival is, what…the Vax equivalent of Special Forces?"

"That's exactly what I'm suggesting."

The general snorted. "We saw him get hurt. He's not immortal."

Senator Johnston shook his head. "Because magic doesn't seem to be anywhere else in the galaxy but Earth and Oriceran, but our boy just received a crash course in it. For all we know, his symbiont might be able to adapt even faster than Brownstone's."

The National Security Advisor pinched the bridge of his nose. "What about the delivery of a nuclear device? Even if we can't trust getting a plane over there, we could send a briefcase nuke over with a few soldiers. Have them arm up, and get the Oricerans to teleport them away after they prime the device."

"Absolutely not," Ambassador Yona replied, her face tight with rage. "A nuclear weapon risks breaking the Great Treaty."

"It's not, strictly speaking, strategic-level magic."

"It's the same level of damage."

Senator Johnston smiled. "I'd offer a suggestion, Madame Ambassador. We have one asset who is far more likely to be able to defeat the Vax: James Brownstone. Since he's not the one stirring up trouble, he might be useful to end it. We can't order him over there, but I know enough about him that if we tap him on the shoulder and let him know a Vax is in town, he'll want to come and give the new guy a little California hello."

Ambassador Yona sighed and shook her head. "That's an even worse idea. We don't have the trust in James Brownstone that you do."

"So I've noticed."

"In addition, even if we presume that he would handle the Vax, he is still a dangerous man who has interfered with the sovereign ruling line of at least one Oriceran race." Ambassador Yona raised her hand and whispered, a soft melody emerging. The image of a Drow with stark white hair and jet-black skin appeared. "If he returns, who knows who might begin to worry? Or how they'll react?"

Senator Johnston nodded toward the Drow. "My understanding is that the Drow don't hold that against him. They're the ones who chose to depose their queen. Brownstone was just a tool for that."

Ambassador Yona gave him a condescending look. "You don't understand the delicate balance on Oriceran. The Great Treaty and other lesser treaties bind everything together well enough that we've managed to avoid the same perpetual warfare that has plagued your planet for the last ten thousand years. The initial opening of the gates has already rendered things unstable. Every additional element of complexity risks damaging that careful balance."

She shook her head. "No James Brownstone." She took

a deep breath. "But it doesn't matter. We didn't come to ask for your help. We came to make it clear we were going to use everything short of strategic-level magic to stop him. Even if we've had some failures, we have a few other options still available. I shall keep you abreast of the situation. With any luck, this unpleasantness will soon be behind us."

"I hope that's true, Madame Ambassador, but unfortunately, I don't think it will be," Senator Johnston replied. He leaned back and shook his head.

The Oricerans might not want James Brownstone involved, but the senator had long since assumed the bounty hunter would have to be. It wouldn't be long, he suspected, before he would have to go have a little chat with the man.

Brownstone's the easy part. That Shepherd bastard always seems to know what's going on. He's going to knock on my door soon, and probably ask if he can sneak a nuke of his own over to Oriceran. Earth, Oriceran, Vax, and the Alliance: four different players. Let's just see if we can get through the next few days without an interdimensional and intergalactic war starting.

CHAPTER SIX

J ames smiled as he stepped into the Leanan Sidhe. The main bar was in a slightly different location, and the new tables were a slightly different color, but someone who hadn't visited it before wouldn't have known it had been half-destroyed in a battle only a few months ago.

Fucking Fortis. You should have just left well enough alone. If you had, you would still be alive.

The thick crowd also proved that no one present worried about any danger. Even though the official cover story was that James had taken on cartel assassins rather than government agents, he had worried that business would drop off. Most people, he presumed, wouldn't want to drink in a place where they might get shot.

James looked at a charred piece of wood hanging on the wall above a brass plaque.

This is a piece of the original bar destroyed in the battle between James Brownstone and the cartel hitmen.

The date of his battle with Fortis was inscribed beneath.

A couple of college kids with USC shirts stood next to the plaque, taking selfies with their phones in increasingly outlandish poses.

James shook his head as he proceeded toward the back and the crowd parted for him by instinct. The pub was one of the few places he could go where most people didn't demand stupid shit like autographs or selfies with him, but he'd been drinking at the place since before he had become famous, even if he didn't hit the pub nearly as often anymore.

The Professor was in his usual spot, his cheeks already red and a half-empty mug of beer in hand. James sat across from him without waiting for an invitation.

James used to spend a lot of time in the place, but things had changed. *He* had changed, but that didn't mean he trusted or respected the Professor any less. Some things never changed.

"Good evening, lad." The Professor offered him a warm smile. "I didn't know you were coming in. I'm assuming because you didn't call, this isn't about work." He sounded intrigued by the possibility.

James shook his head. "Nah. Shay doesn't want any jobs until after the honeymoon. Try to avoid asking her, even if you need top-level talent. She's all in as far as this wedding shit goes."

"I'm not one to stand between a woman and the wedding of her dreams, particularly when that woman is as lethal as Miz Carson." The Professor took a sip of his beer. "If you're not here for work, are you here for a drink?" A wicked grin spread across his face. "Or are you finally ready to take another crack at being the Bard of Filth? We're not having a contest tonight, but I could be persuaded to have an exhibition match."

"Not that shit either. Never that shit." James grimaced. "Something more important. Wedding shit."

Confusion took over the Professor's face. "What about the wedding?"

"I need a best man." James shrugged. "It might sound weird, but you're the first person who comes to mind."

The Professor rubbed his chin. "A best man, which means I'd have to give a speech extolling your virtues. Aye, that sounds like a lot of work."

James grunted. "There's an open fucking bar."

"Excellent, lad." The Professor raised his mug. "Then I'm willing to work."

James chuckled. "Good to know your priorities are always the same."

The next morning, James settled in at the conference table at Camp Brownstone. He didn't typically bother going to meetings anymore, but since Trey was in town, he thought it was a good time to check in with everyone. Especially since they'd had a few new hires in the last several months.

Trey sat next to James, while Maria and Staff Sergeant Royce sat on the other side of the table.

Maria nodded at James. "I know how much you hate meetings, so I'll get right to the point. Things are going well. Really damned well. I've got very few complaints, and you know me. I like to bitch about stuff."

Trey laughed. "That's one way to put it."

Maria smiled. "How else am I going to describe it? We've got steady and consistent captures in LA, and the Vegas teams have been cleaning up, too. We're steam-rolling the bastards out there."

Royce nodded. "None of the new recruits have washed out, and I've stepped up training. We've got a good team of men and women, with more experience than Trey and his guys had when they came in. I'm surprised by how well they've adapted to how we do things here."

"Why is that?" James asked with a frown. "I figure guys with more experience would have less trouble than gang members."

"The agency culture is...particular. Some people might not want to work next to ex-gang members or, for Vegas rotations, take orders from them. Even though we've started adding more of a formal chain of command, at the end of the day, Trey and Maria are the people calling the shots for field operations, and it's important that everyone respect that." Royce shrugged. "But it hasn't been an issue, and no one's had a problem with me coordinating training. It's like we're a bounty-hunting machine."

James nodded, satisfied. These reports were consistent with everything he'd been hearing and reading, but it was good to sit down and look people in the eye as they related what was going on. It helped ensure that no one was holding back because they were afraid the Granite Ghost would attempt his own brand of "training."

Maria frowned slightly. "We've had to expand outside

of LA and Orange County at times, just to make sure we have enough revenue, given the number of bounty hunters we have, but that hasn't been a big problem. Plenty of scum in SoCal."

Trey grinned. "You can always send the overflow to Las Vegas. It might not be LA, but they're punching above their weight in terms of freaks. I've got the Mafia nice and tamed for now, but that don't mean it's a safe town, and it'll be a long time before it is."

"It doesn't have to be," James replied. "And if it gets too safe, then we just spread out more. If we need to travel for bounties, we can do that, but I don't want to grow the agency too much." He grunted. "No shit where we have branch offices all over or whatever, but I don't mind grabbing assholes in other cities. It's good to hear all this from you guys, though. It makes what I have to say next easier."

Trey's grin turned to a frown. "I don't like the sound of that shit, big man."

James shook his head. "It's nothing bad. I've been talking a lot with Shay and Alison, and I think that after the wedding I'm gonna dial shit down even more than I have."

"Meaning what?" Maria asked with a curious look on her face.

Royce didn't say anything as he watched the conversation unfold. The ex-Marine was always ready to follow orders and react to the situation with professionalism.

"Meaning I'm semi-retiring," James replied. "Not fully retiring, but like I said, semi-retiring. I want to begin planning to open a barbeque restaurant."

Trey whistled. "Damn, big man. I kind of knew this day

was coming, but James Brownstone deciding he's done is a big-ass deal. It's the fucking end of an era."

"Not really." James nodded at Trey. "You've been bagging level fours by yourself lately, and a lot of the teams have done well, too. The agency doesn't need me. You've got shit completely handled. I'm overkill at this point."

"Not that I disagree, but I do have concerns." Maria sighed. "I'm ex-AET, so I know all too well what non-magicals need to take down enhanced threats. I'm willing to say that our top teams here could do a great job against any level four, but level fives? I don't think it's a smart play. There's too much of a risk."

James grunted. "Like I said, semi-retired, not fully retired. I figure for level fives, if they're dumbshits enough to come to LA or Vegas, that means they want an appointment with me. In those cases, you all just concentrate on finding them, and I'll lead the final team to take them down. No reason to go looking for too much trouble. If some level-five fucker wants to jack up Denver or some shit, we can let someone else handle it."

Maria nodded, relief coming to her face. "We could still use a few more magicals, especially on the LA side of things."

"May Wu still might join, but I'm not gonna press her on it. She knows the offer is there." James shrugged. His phone buzzed with an alarm. "Is that pretty much it? If so, I've got some shit I want to talk to Trey about."

Maria stood. "I'm good. I think we're all on the same page, and nothing anyone said is surprising."

Royce stood as well, a mischievous grin on his face.

"I've got a fitness run I want to lead for a few of the guys who are letting themselves go."

Trey rested his elbow on the table and waited.

Maria and Royce departed.

"What's up, big man? Trey asked.

"Yesterday, I asked the Professor to be my best man," James explained.

Trey laughed. "Shit, motherfucker! You're gonna need a whole fucking lake of beer at that wedding if Smite-Williams is showing up."

James chuckled. "Probably, but he's helped me out for my entire career, and in a way, he's my oldest real friend. You aren't offended or shit like that, are you?"

"Nah, but that old drunk being your oldest real friend is kind of sad in a way. Don't matter much. You're marrying a fine-ass babe, so who the fuck needs friends, you know what I'm saying?" Trey winked.

"Yeah." James nodded to the other man. "I still need groomsmen, though. I already asked Mack, and he agreed. Now I'm asking you. You're not gonna have to do all the usher shit. There'll be too many people, so Shay's gonna hire professional ushers, and she told me to get five groomsmen to match the number of bridesmaids she's going to have." He started ticking off fingers. "Maria, Kara, Janelle, Bella, and Alison. We're still deciding on if we're gonna have a flower girl and a ringbearer and shit. I want Thomas to bring the rings, but Shay disagrees."

Trey laughed. "Seriously, big man?"

"He's a smart dog." James shrugged.

"Your wedding."

James lifted his other hand to tick off more fingers.

"The Professor, you, Mack, and Tyler. Maria's gonna ask him for me. Still trying to decide on the fifth groomsman."

Trey eyed James like he'd lost his mind. "You want Tyler to be one of your groomsmen?"

"Yeah. It'll make him feel special and shit. He can be annoying at times, but he's fed me a lot of good information over the years, and it's obvious Maria wants to marry him, so I might as well feed him a bone. It's good for the agency."

"Sure, okay." Trey looked down a for a moment, his brow furrowed. "Look, big man, this is gonna sound weird, but I think you should only have four groomsmen."

"Why?"

Trey lifted his head. "Because I want to leave a spot in memory of Shorty. Kind of a way to honor him. I know I ain't have the right to ask you that, given that it's supposed to be the happiest day of your life and shit…"

James shook his head. "It's fine. You're right. Leaving a spot for Shorty's not a bad idea, and if he were still alive, he'd probably be the fifth man anyway."

Trey's expression brightened. "Thanks. I don't think you know how much this means to me."

"You'd be surprised. I won't ever forget him."

"You don't ever forget anything."

James snorted. "All the more reason. Thanks for the suggestion. That's all I had to ask about."

Trey stood and fluffed his lapels. "You sure? I'm heading back to Vegas tonight, so if there's anything else you need while I'm in town, let me know."

"Nah. I'm good." James shrugged. "Just keep doing what you're doing."

Trey headed toward the door with a smile on his face.

Looks like I can finally just go ahead with my life, James thought. *No crazy-ass aliens or CIA hunters after me. It might still be a few months until the wedding, but it'll be good to get everyone used to shit before then.*

Nothing on Earth can fuck this shit up now.

CHAPTER SEVEN

Sentry 8224 sighed as he reviewed the holographic display of the grainy video clip on his ocular implant and leaned back in the comfortable chair. If anyone was recording or watching him, they would see nothing but a human man seemingly distracted at a desk in his home office.

I can't believe I'm reduced to this. I knew Johnston was hiding something, but this?

All the advanced technology of the Nine Systems Alliance, and the Shepherd still found himself almost completely thwarted by the strange combination of primitive Earth computer systems and the much more concerning magic, but he hadn't failed totally. A small nanoprobe had managed to infiltrate the meeting with the Oriceran ambassador.

The probe hadn't been able to collect any audio and had mysteriously failed after a few minutes, but the Shepherd had gotten what he needed: evidence of the arrival of another Vax. It was as he feared and expected. He had hoped it might take years instead of months, but in a disturbing way, he wasn't surprised.

Aiyn was right in her own way. Now it's up to us to make sure her sacrifice wasn't pointless.

The Shepherd tapped his silver AllBand on his wrist a few times and waited. The device buzzed.

"Report," ordered a harsh voice through one of his auditory implants: Fleet Commander Laralan.

The officer currently commanded a four-ship fleet hidden in the outer fringes of the Solar System. The Shepherd knew that some had challenged his request for the fleet. They thought it was a waste of resources, but now, he had all the proof he needed. He only wished he had even more ships available.

"Sentry 8224 reporting verification of a Vax on Oriceran," the Shepherd responded. "I'll be transmitting the recording, but from what I can tell, it's Purifier or Destroyer class."

The commander sighed. "Even though we knew this was coming, that doesn't make it any less concerning. Oriceran, though? It is my understanding that the humans have insisted you deal with the Oricerans through them. That will make things more complicated."

"That's true, sir. In order to maintain good relationships with the relevant human governments, I've agreed to that situation for the moment." The Shepherd transmitted the image data from his probe. "But that doesn't change the fact that the intelligence I've collected clearly shows a Vax destroying an Oriceran town."

"I see," the commander replied. "That might explain why we've never been able to find a point of origin. Maybe we've been wrong, and the Vax *aren't* in this galaxy. From what you've told me, Oriceran might not be in this galaxy."

"Neither the humans nor the Oricerans are completely certain of that point, sir, to be honest. They often refer to Oriceran being in a different dimension, but they haven't firmly ruled out that it might simply be far away in conventional space-time. The fact that the Vax can portal to the planet suggests that might be the case."

"Damn," Fleet Commander Laralan replied. "I'm watching the recording now. If they understood properly what they had been dealing with, they might have had some small chance, but from what I see, all they did was make the Purifier stronger. What sort of countermeasures do you think will come next?"

"I'm unsure, sir, but I do know the Oricerans are reluctant to use magic equivalent to strategic-scale weapons because of their history. I'm having some issues acquiring real-time intelligence on this matter. Unfortunately, the humans don't trust the Alliance implicitly."

"I don't understand much about magic, but what little I do understand suggests we have little chance of getting our ships to Oriceran."

The Shepherd didn't respond immediately. He looked up at the ceiling, trying to think of the best course of action, but the same idea kept returning.

"Even if the Oricerans were willing and able to generate a portal of the necessary size, I doubt they would agree to allow the Alliance to orbit four warships above their planet, sir," the Shepherd explained. "But I'm at least going to ask. They've already seen what a Vax can do, and it might make them more inclined to take such an offer."

Commander Laralan growled in frustration. "The monster gets to lay waste to a world, and there's nothing we can do about it if they don't let us go there."

"I don't believe that's the case, sir."

"You don't?"

The Shepherd stood and walked over to his window, staring out into the densely packed buildings of the city. "Yes, sir. If this had been about Brownstone summoning the Vax, they would have appeared on Earth directly, not on Oriceran. That's an important distinction."

Commander Laralan snorted. "What good does it do us now? It doesn't matter if Brownstone called the Purifier. It's there. I don't know why they didn't follow their standard attack patterns, but now it's only important that we respond."

"That's just it, sir." The Shepherd allowed himself a triumphant smile even if he was the only one there to know about it. "My investigations, combined with what little Brownstone and Senator Johnston have passed along, suggest that Brownstone might not have originally arrived on Earth. I believe he was originally on Oriceran, and somehow portaled to Earth as a young child. I also would estimate the unusual Vax behavior is because this is some kind of recovery mission."

"And what do you base that on?"

"There was a similar incident about twenty years ago," the Shepherd explained. "It was on a small border planet. The Vax Forerunner there initiated some conflicts and summoned the Vanguard, but there was a successful psionic attack against the Forerunner. The locals didn't dare use it until they were desperate, but it worked. The

Vax started acting erratically, and it wasn't long after that a Purifier arrived to destroy the local Vax and continue razing the planet with Destroyers. The locals attempted the same attack again, but it failed. The Purifier had already assimilated the symbionts of the slain Vax."

Commander Laralan let out a small grunt of approval. "You think it's looking for Brownstone, then?"

"Yes. If this was about conquering Oriceran, it would have already summoned the Destroyers or the Vanguard. I'm sure they'll come to Oriceran eventually, but I think it's a secondary priority."

Commander Laralan blew out a breath. "If it's seeking Brownstone, that means it'll eventually come to Earth."

"Yes, sir, and, if that's the case, we have a chance, even without the Oricerans agreeing to anything. I would recommend that we no longer worry about concealing the fleet. You'll need to be in position when the creature comes over."

"Duly noted. Very well, I'll leave it to you to smooth over the diplomatic issues. Contact me immediately if you become aware of any new intelligence."

The AllBand buzzed with the termination of the link.

The Shepherd folded his hands behind his back. He didn't need magic or Alliance technology to guess where the Vax would arrive. If it was looking for Brownstone, it would come to Los Angeles soon enough.

Yona folded her hands in her lap and peered through the scrying window. Some dangers couldn't be allowed to exist. If they couldn't beat the Vax Purifier without strategic-level magic, then there was one major option remaining.

The elf watched as a portal opened. A group of elves emerged and spread out in a half-circle. They had positioned themselves a few hundred yards away from the Purifier. An illusionary wall of trees concealed their position. It would all be over soon enough.

The Purifier continued advancing on its previous course. Currently, the monster was striding through the woods, ignoring the few animals nearby. Only fortune had spared additional victims other than the guardsmen and the second team. The Vax had come close to another city, but not turned toward it. If he traveled long enough in a straight line, he would hit another city, but he would have to cross a sea first.

Everything the US government had passed along about the Vax suggested they were a conquering and destructive species. The Purifier had already proven the latter, but his refusal to lay waste to any additional towns suggested there was some other goal in mind.

Where is he going? Is there something we're missing?

Ambassador Yona shook her head. It didn't matter. He couldn't hurt anyone on Oriceran trapped in the World in Between, and he would be delivered there in moments.

Lines of light surrounded the elves, and complex glyphs appeared in the air in front of them as they murmured their incantations. The Purifier stopped moving and turned in their direction.

He can sense them?

Yona's heart sped up, and her lips parted. They couldn't restrain the Vax. The current plan had to work.

The Purifier marched straight toward the illusionary trees, his movement slow, steady, and indefatigable. There was no sense of urgency in his steps, nor did he raise his arms. The deadly shoulder appendages in his armor twitched but didn't fire.

This can work. He's not reacting quickly enough.

The elves continued their ritual. Swirling energy flowed in front of them, still hidden by the illusion. The spell was working.

Yona let out a sigh of relief. They had worried so much over nothing. The loss of life at Alazi was a tragedy, but the most important thing was to protect Oriceran without risking the disruption of the status quo or the Great Treaty. The Vax monster was threatening to do just that, threatening them in a way that no one since Rhazdon had done, and he would be delivered to a terrible fate.

The illusion disappeared. The Purifier broke into a jog, but he still didn't fire.

Your arrogance will be your downfall, monster.

A dark hole appeared above the Vax. Air rushed into the hole, and a few stray branches flew inside. The Purifier stopped, straining against the force trying to pull it into the deadly portal. A pulse of green energy blasted from the armor, and the portal vanished.

Yona gasped. Impossible.

The Purifier leapt through the air, raising his arms. He crashed through branches as he rained down energy blasts on the elves. Several of them died in an instant. All their magic and attention had been focused on the World in Between ritual, not defense.

The survivors managed to summon their shields as the Purifier drew closer. He landed with a blade down, cleaving another elf in two. His other arm and the shoulder appendages continued to fire.

Shields saved a few elves from the first attack, but the Purifier sliced and stabbed, his blades piercing their magic with ease. One elf managed to escape with the help of a gust of air.

The Purifier fired both appendages and his arm blades, and several volleys of green energy struck the fleeing man. The third volley pierced his shield and ripped into his back. He tumbled to the ground, dead before he hit.

Yona stared at the image wide-eyed. Thousands of years of life had been destroyed in moments. The monster turned his featureless helmeted head back and forth a few times before resuming his march.

There must be some other way to stop this monster.

CHAPTER EIGHT

S hay leaned against the headboard of the bed, her legs underneath the blanket as she swiped through images on her phone. A single lamp illuminated the bedroom. "I still can't get over what you did."

James grunted as he finished brushing his teeth and put his toothbrush in its holder. "Huh? What are you talking about? Taking a shower and brushing my teeth?"

"I was just reviewing the guest list." Shay held up her phone. "And having to add Frank Altieri plus eight reminded me of your...I don't even know what to call it. Genius? Insanity? Strange-ass plan?"

James shrugged and walked toward his side of the bed. "I was there anyway, and it's a good idea."

"I know. As strange as it sounds, I agree with you. Since you're giving Heather extra time off, I've got Peyton tracking down the best contact info for all the major organized crime leaders. We'll just mail them invitations. It saves you time." Shay winked. "And here I thought the whole idea was a joke, but look at you, James Brownstone, doing the ultimate power play over the entirety of the Los Angeles underworld."

James crawled into bed with a frown. "I'm just trying to be smart about this shit and save myself trouble down the line, but is it going to be a problem? We're talking about adding a lot of people. Can we find a place that big? Maybe I should have kept it to mob leader plus one."

Shay shook her head. She tapped her phone a few times before turning it around. The phone displayed an aerial photograph of a forested island with a large white mansion in the center, a paved road leading to an almost-as-large beach cabana. "I was thinking of renting this island for the wedding."

"We're gonna rent an island?" James didn't hide the doubt in his tone. "For our wedding?"

Shay grinned. "You think we should buy it instead? It's surprisingly cheap, as far as islands go."

"What the fuck would we do with an island?"

Shay flipped her phone around and started swiping again. "I could put warehouses there."

"Not very convenient," James replied. "You gonna fly to an island every time you need to grab some gear?"

"I could store my really dangerous artifacts there." Shay shrugged. "Okay, no buying the island. We'll rent it, so it doesn't matter how many people we invite. Groomsmen, check. Bridesmaids, check. Food, check. Shit, this wedding is starting to come together. Hiring that wedding planner really helped."

"Good to hear." James nodded. "Anything that doesn't involve me having to do shit sounds good to me."

Shay's grin turned predatory "Still need to figure out a

honeymoon. If you don't give me input, maybe I'll do something evil."

"What's evil?" James asked.

"Like book us a trip to a vegan resort."

"Now that's just fucking twisted." James shook his head. "No fucking vegan resorts. Not vegetarian, either. I get that there might not be American-style barbeque there, but I at least want access to grilled and sauced meat. That is non-negotiable."

Shay laughed. "I'll take that under advisement, James."

He frowned at a sudden realization. "What about Alison?"

"What about her? She's happy to be a bridesmaid."

James shook his head. "No, I'm talking about after the wedding. We gonna just leave her home alone with Thomas?"

"Yes, the poor, poor child. You think she can't survive a few weeks by herself even though she's almost an adult, has powerful magic and has participated in hunting down bounties?" Shay smirked. "If you're that worried, just ask if she can stay with someone when you're gone—Mack or Charlyce or Heather. Whoever."

"Okay, that works." James laid his head on the pillow, his thoughts churning with everything that was coming up in the next several months. "I still have to figure out the wedding ring, but I've got an idea."

"Oh? This ought to be interesting. Let's hear it."

"That *lele* in Romania gave me a diamond, right? It's just sitting around gathering dust. I'm gonna take it to some jeweler and have them cut it down and make it into the ring. I figure some diamond that I got for helping take down a three-headed dragon in a haunted forest is pretty fucking epic as a wedding ring."

Shay looked thoughtful and nodded. "I can't disagree. Not as functional as my engagement ring, but stacking shields doesn't usually work anyway. You're gonna take point on that?"

"Yeah. I'll handle it. Do you want it to be big or small?"

"Big!" Shay cackled. "I want everyone in my department to be, 'Ack, Shay your wedding ring is blinding me. I have to put on some sunglasses.' Screw being classy. I'm going straight diva with that thing."

"Might be hard to fight with it," James observed.

"I'll take it off when I need to kill someone. Easy." Shay set her phone on her nightstand and stuck her hands behind her head. "It's weird when I think about it, all the way back to that first raid together. I never saw anything like this coming."

"Lots of shit I didn't see coming. I never thought I'd have a kid and a wife." James stared up at the ceiling, oddly soothed by the patterns in the paint. "Or, shit, semi-retiring from bounty hunting."

"Are you worried at all?"

James shook his head. "Nah. It feels…right. That's part of the reason I want those mobsters and shit there, so I can put everyone on notice that just because I'm not doing it full-time doesn't mean I can't come out and kick some ass if I need to."

"Not just because you like seeing them squirm?"

"That shit's fun, too." James shrugged and grinned. "I was never very interested in the Brownstone Effect. Being a bounty hunter was just the only thing I could figure to do with my skills. I wasn't trying to clean up the city."

"What we want and what happens are two different things." Shay nodded toward her phone. "Maybe that's why I'm picking an island for the wedding."

"What do you mean?"

"That was my big plan, remember? To make enough money to disappear to an island. I wasn't supposed to be getting into a relationship, or having a new daughter and a new life." Shay chuckled quietly. "Or friends who are actual friends, and not the kind of bitches who'll kill me in my own kitchen." She sighed. "It's kind of weird. It's almost like when I couldn't trust people, I knew what to expect, and now, living a more normal life is simultaneously more relaxing and more stressful at the same time. I actually have to give a fuck about people."

"Because life is more complicated. You can't have friends and shit without things being complicated." James sat up. "I get that now. I don't know, maybe if Father Thomas hadn't died, I wouldn't be so fucked up."

Shay gave James a sideways glance. "You're a genetically-modified alien whose parents sent you to Oriceran when you were a little kid to prevent you from becoming the bitch of a biotechnological symbiont with delusions of grandeur. Sorry, James, you didn't stand a chance of coming out normal, but you're doing pretty well, all things considered."

"There's something else we need to talk about." James frowned. "We should have discussed it earlier when I proposed."

"What?"

"Kids."

"Alison?" Shay's expression turned confused.

James shook his head. "Kids in general. I'm not sure I can have any. I might have been genetically modified by Whispy to be more human, but I'm not human. Are you okay with that?"

Shay laughed. "I wasn't exactly eager to get pregnant anytime soon. We've got a perfectly great kid in Alison. I'm not really going to worry about it." Her smile turned to a look of concern. "Are you concerned about it?"

"I don't know." James stared down at his hands. They weren't as calloused as he was used to, a side-effect of Whispy's regeneration modifications. "I'm satisfied with the family I have. I've got two great women my life and a great dog, even if he is a whiny little bitch when it comes to wanting my barbeque sauce."

"I'm feeling good." Shay slipped underneath the covers and turned off the lamp. "And you should, too. I think our luck's turning around."

"Meaning?"

"I think as long as I avoid any tomb raids, we won't have any trouble. Pretty much all the threats from my tomb raiding days have been taken care of." Shay let out a contented sigh. "Even the ones I didn't know about. I figure if we mind our business, the universe will take care of the rest for us."

"And if the universe decides to cause trouble?"

Shay turned on her side, an evil look on her face. "If someone fucks up our wedding, you better blow up a city to punish them."

James grunted. "I'll keep that in mind."

CHAPTER NINE

H*ere we go again,* Senator Johnston thought.

He picked up his coffee mug and took a sip. It was too damned early in the morning for another meeting, but the Oriceran failure to stop the advancing Vax had turned the situation from a diplomatic to a potential national security issue.

Ambassador Yona slumped in her chair, pale since she'd explained what happened to the team.

"You've got no choice," the National Security Advisor declared. "You've got to release strategic-level magic. Magically nuke the bastard. Nuke him until he glows, then nuke him again. Leave a crater so deep, it'd take him years to crawl out even if he did survive."

Yona slowly lifted her head, pity in her eyes. "You humans think you understand destruction. You think your great world wars and your nuclear weapons have made you the gods of death, but you know nothing of real destruction. You know nothing of the kind of war that scars an entire planet. Of the kind of war that etches itself in memories for the rest of existence."

"Be that as it may, Ambassador, that Vax will kill more people. Worrying about your treaty and some war that happened thousands of years ago when you have a clear and present danger seems short-sighted. You need to act quickly to take the monster out. You know its location, so do what you need to do."

Ambassador Yona shook her head. "King Oriceran has made his will clear. We will not risk abrogating the treaty. We won't risk Oriceran's total destruction out of panic. You mock the idea of worrying about a war that happened in the distant past, but it is our respect for that past which has prevented another such war."

The National Security Advisor scoffed. "How many people need to die before you buy a clue? I might be a short-sighted human, but at least I can see the truth."

Several other people at the table winced. Senator Johnston sighed.

Yona's face contorted in rage. "How dare you, human! Most of the Oricerans who have died at the hands of this creature had lived for centuries. We are keenly aware of the loss of every such being, and I won't be lectured by a human on the matter."

Senator Johnston cleared his throat. "If I might interject?"

Everyone swung their heads toward him except Ambassador Yona, who kept glaring at the National Security Advisor.

"I actually agree with Ambassador Yona," Senator Johnston explained.

The National Security Advisor snorted. "Really? I expected better of you, Angus."

"Yes. I understand where you're coming from, but they just lost an entire team of elves trying to send him to the World in Between, and that's not counting the other teams they've lost. For all we know, the Vax might be immune to even a strategic-level spell." Senator Johnston gestured toward the ambassador. "So nuking a bunch of the Oriceran countryside to stop one Vax might not only be overkill, but pointless overkill. Besides, you heard what she said in the briefing. The Vax keeps passing up opportunities to take out towns, and at least there are no significant population centers in the way before he hits the ocean. If they evacuate the smaller areas in between, that means almost no casualties."

The National Security Advisor looked at Ambassador Yona and Senator Johnston with a confused expression. "So, what...your big plan is for him to drown? I'm willing to bet the kind of aliens who send super-soldier killing machines across the galaxy understand they might occasionally run into an ocean or two."

Ambassador Yona took a deep breath and slowly let it out. "The Vax won't go to the ocean."

"Why are you so sure?"

The elf's face twitched. "Because contrary to what you seem to believe, we're not naïve fools. Since the destruction of Alazi, the creature's course has been unerring. It's going somewhere in particular."

The National Security Advisor nodded. "But where?"

"We've been examining the areas intersecting its general course," Ambassador Yona explained. "We've been looking for unusual magic or anything that would explain the creature's goal on Oriceran."

"He's searching, and he has a trail," Senator Johnston suggested. "I'm guessing it's probably searching for Brownstone."

"That's our belief as well. We did find something: an area with unusual portal resonance. The Vax has been directly marching toward that area."

A quiet murmur swept the table.

"I'm not an expert on magic, Ambassador," Senator Johnston replied. "Could you clarify the implications of that for me?"

The elf frowned. "I would if we had a better understanding of it ourselves. The resonance is like nothing we've encountered before, and there's only one other place on Oriceran we've been able to find that has a similar resonance."

Senator Johnston sighed. "Let me guess. Right outside of Alazi, I presume."

Ambassador Yona nodded.

The National Security Advisor looked at the two of them. "It's looking for wherever Brownstone portaled onto Oriceran? What good does that do? He's not on Oriceran anymore."

"Because, sir," Senator Johnston explained, "Brownstone eventually ended up on Earth. I'm guessing that once the Vax finds that area, he'll go to where Brownstone next appeared."

"Which is where, exactly?"

"Los Angeles."

The National Security Advisor gritted his teeth and

glared at Ambassador Yona. "We can't let that thing into a major city. I understand the losses you've suffered, but we're not talking hundreds here. We're talking millions of people at risk. You *have* to nuke the bastard." He looked at Johnston. "Or is this some sort of spy thing? He's going to hook up with Brownstone, and they'll attack together?"

Senator Johnston scoffed. "James Brownstone could have brought the pain without a rude family member. No, I suspect this is not all that different from what any oppressive, violent government does to a defector when they have a chance. I suspect this is an assassination. It just so happens that this assassin isn't bothering to be subtle."

The Chairman of the Joint Chiefs slammed a fist on the table. "Then we should take Brownstone and stick him in the middle of the desert. We wait for the Vax to come through, and we drop our own nukes on him."

Senator Johnston chuckled. "We start setting off nukes or strategic-level magic on this side, and it won't only be the Oricerans we have to worry about. I'd rather not accidentally start a nuclear war, gentlemen."

The National Security Advisor frowned. "We'd be nuking ourselves. We can even tell them why."

"You tell other countries that we're dropping nukes because of an alien invasion, and I guarantee they toss a few nukes our way too. Next thing you know, we've done the Vax's work for him. I don't know about you, but I don't think there will be much need for a senator in a post-apocalyptic radioactive wasteland."

Ambassador Yona watched Senator Johnston with an appreciative look on her face.

The Chairman of the Joint Chiefs pointed up. "What about asking the Alliance for help?"

"We don't know what they might do. For all we know, they might decide they have to boil the Earth to get the Vax. Besides, if we go hat in hand to aliens for help, they'll think we're weak, and that has negotiating implications going forward. We need to prove that we can defend ourselves."

The National Security Advisor shook his head. "We can't sit here and do nothing. We need to—"

"It won't work, by the way," Senator Johnston interrupted. "The bait plan."

"What? You think it's immune to nuclear weapons?"

"I don't know about that, but you're missing the obvious." Senator Johnston gestured toward Ambassador Yona. "Our Vax friend is ignoring cities now, but when he appeared, he was in a city, and he destroyed it. Even if we can lure him out to the desert by sticking James Brownstone there, there is still the distinct possibility the Vax will end up in the middle of LA. If he does, he'll probably spend at least a little time sightseeing in an unpleasant manner before he chases after James Brownstone."

The National Security Advisor scrubbed a hand over his face. "Then what do we do? If the Oricerans can't or won't stop him and he does come over, I don't think a few Marines will be enough."

"We need to give him what he wants," Senator Johnston suggested. "If James Brownstone doesn't leave LA, that'll keep the Vax there, and James Brownstone is our best bet for beating this thing without nukes or strategic-level magic."

Everyone stared at Senator Johnston as if tentacles had popped out of his head.

"And what?" the Chairman of the Joint Chiefs asked. "We let this happen in LA? First of all, we don't even know if Brownstone can win."

"No, we don't," Senator Johnston replied. "But he's had a long time and a lot of strange creatures to adapt to. I'd give him good odds. Plus, a man defending his home is always going to fight harder than a man coming from the outside to mess with him. I think we at least give him the chance."

"And if he fails?" The Chairman stared at him, his eyebrow raised in challenge.

"Then I suggest we use both nuclear weapons and strategic-level spells. We drop everything we have until there's nothing left."

Ambassador Yona snorted. "You would kill millions of your own people to destroy one creature? You yourself just mentioned a risk of global war."

"I'm only offering that as a final suggestion. Maybe we can toss him in a trench or something if we get lucky, but if your people couldn't send him to the World in Between, I doubt any clever spells or tricks we can come up with would work." Senator Johnston smiled disarmingly. "And, no, I don't intend for anyone other than James Brownstone to be at risk if at all possible."

The National Security Advisor returned to looking confused. "How are you going to manage that? Try to lock them in with shield spells?"

"I suspect the Vax could get through that. No, the

easiest way to ensure no one is hurt is to make sure they aren't there to begin with."

"Huh?"

Senator Johnston gestured widely. "I suggest we completely evacuate Los Angeles and Orange Counties."

Stunned silence gripped the table. If they did what he suggested, they would be undertaking one of the greatest mass evacuations in human history, affecting tens of millions of people. It might even be the largest.

"That's insane," the National Security Advisor objected. "And if we start to evacuate them because of the Vax, what's to stop all those other countries you mentioned lobbing their nukes to stop an alien invasion? Make up your mind, Angus."

"I have no intention of announcing to the world that an invasion is taking place." Senator Johnston smiled. "I'm here in this room because the President has invested me with unusual authority in many matters related to the non-Oriceran extraterrestrial issue, and it is in this capacity that I recommend we recruit James Brownstone to fight the Vax, and we evacuate the area to ensure minimum collateral damage."

"And you're going to do all of that without admitting the reason?"

Senator Johnston nodded. "That is the idea."

"How?"

Senator Johnston laughed. "By doing what politicians do best: lying."

CHAPTER TEN

A couple of hours later, Senator Johnston was going through contingency plans on his computer when there was a knock on his door. He wasn't expecting anyone, and he didn't like being surprised.

Plastering on a smile, the senator reached for the desk drawer where he kept a .38 loaded with anti-magic bullets. "Come on in."

The door opened to reveal a handsome dark-haired man in a suit—Sentry 8224, or as he liked humans to call him, Corey.

"Well, now," Senator Johnston offered. "This is unexpected. I would have thought you would have made an appointment like you did in the past." He kept his hand on the gun beneath his desk.

"I apologize for approaching you directly, but the circumstances required it. This one time we can't sit around playing games and discussing possibilities is during a crisis." The Shepherd tapped the silver bracelet he wore.

He'd admitted it was a technological device in the past when directly asked.

"I'm a US senator, my alien friend. I'm always dealing with a crisis. Would you care to be more specific in this instance?"

Corey sneered and shook his head. "Your flippancy is amusing, considering your planet is on the verge of destruction."

Senator Johnston chuckled. "Now you sound like a passionate young person. Crisis this. Crisis that. Again, what are you talking about?"

Determining what Corey knew would help ascertain what sort of intelligence the alien could collect when the US government kept information from him.

"There's a Vax Purifier on Oriceran right now," Corey declared. "It has already destroyed one town. Don't try to deny it. I know it. I've seen it."

"I haven't denied anything." Senator Johnston tossed his gun back in the drawer and ignored the flick of the alien's eyes toward the side of the desk. "I just wanted to make sure we were about to discuss the same issue. It doesn't hurt to be careful. After all, it's not like I want to accidentally pass on classified information to a…foreign national."

Corey narrowed his eyes. "This is an unusual situation. The Forerunner didn't summon the Vanguard, but that doesn't make this situation any less dangerous regardless of the slight shift in Vax tactics. It's not too late, though. You can request formal, open assistance from the Alliance. Even if this creates some difficulties with our open-contact protocols, we can help, especially if the Oricerans can generate a portal large enough to allow ships to go to their world." A forced smile took over his face. "I understand there are political ramifications pertaining to the use of certain types of weapons for both the Oricerans and your Earth governments. We could provide a way out of that conundrum. We could take out the Vax without you using any of your weapons or spells of mass destruction."

Senator Johnston snorted and narrowed his eyes. The alien was always underestimating him. Advanced technology might have let Corey spy on him somehow, but he needed better info when dealing with a detail-oriented man.

"Ships?" Senator Johnston asked. "Now that's an interesting word choice, because I'm fairly certain that when we last discussed this, you told us there was only one small ship present in our solar system."

"A Vax Purifier has appeared, and you're quibbling over sovereignty?" Corey shook his head. "Pride will lead to nothing but your planet becoming a burned-out husk."

Senator Johnston leaned forward and folded his hands. "Let me lay it out for you, my alien friend: even *if* the Oricerans could portal over some Alliance ship from orbit to above Oriceran, which is a big *if*, considering the limits magic has when you get away from the surface of the planet, I highly doubt they would do it. They're even more skittish about weapons of mass destruction than we are. So give it up. It's a dream." He shrugged. "Besides, neither Oriceran nor Earth needs the Alliance's help."

Corey scoffed. "Then how do you intend to stop the Purifier? The Oricerans have already failed, and the fact that we're even having this discussion proves they can't. In every battle, an already strong foe grows stronger."

"It's easy to stop an ultimate weapon."

"How?"

Senator Johnston gestured grandly. "With another ultimate weapon."

"Brownstone?" Corey shook his head in disbelief. "*That's* your big plan? You're just going to throw Brownstone at the Vax?"

"I intend to ask him politely, but I'm not worried. He's already made it clear that he's more than happy to fight any Vax who might arrive. So, you see, your assistance is not needed at this time since we have access to other advanced alien technology."

Corey took a few steps toward Senator Johnston, his face tight. Senator Johnston reached into the drawer and gripped the gun again.

"You don't understand." Corey hissed. "A Forerunner is nothing more than a glorified scout. That's why it calls the Vanguard, and a Purifier is far worse than the Vanguard. It can also summon Destroyers, which are also far worse. James Brownstone can't win, and that's assuming he doesn't betray your planet the first chance he gets."

Senator Johnston clucked his tongue. "Now, now, that's an awful thing to say. I have faith in James Brownstone, far more than I do in the Nine Systems Alliance. Let me make that clear up front."

Something approaching panic covered Corey's face. "Even if Brownstone doesn't join his people, there is still the risk that they can gain access to his adaptation potential. It's bad enough that we have one Vax exposed to magic, and now we have another. Soon, more will come."

He shook his head. "You're forcing the Alliance into a dangerous position."

Senator Johnston frowned. "I'm going to have to ask you to clarify exactly what you mean by that."

"Even setting aside the threat to the lives on Oriceran and Earth, the Alliance can't allow the Vax to successfully invade and adapt to both worlds. We'll do what we have to do, even if you don't agree."

"That sounds like a threat to the ears of this old human."

Corey spun on his heel. "Consider it a warning. We'll do everything we can to minimize collateral damage, but if you won't work with us, we'll have no choice but to solve the problem ourselves." He stepped outside and slammed the office door closed behind him.

Senator Johnston sighed and shook his head. He pulled out his phone to make a call.

I suspected this would happen, and I'm glad we took precautions.

CHAPTER ELEVEN

James pulled out of the gas station onto the street. He often wondered how long it would be before he wasn't able to fuel up his truck anymore. Every year there were fewer gas stations and more charging stations. When he looked around, more electric vehicles filled the road than gas-powered vehicles.

This truck is from a different era.

It wasn't like James could blame his choice of vehicles on being old. He might be closing in on forty, but he had a few years yet. He had always preferred the growl of a nice V8, even when he was a teen. The world might be changing, but there were a few things he wanted to hold onto forever. If magic could exist, he didn't see why a man couldn't own a classic truck.

I'm asking Shay about kids, but we still don't even know how long I'm gonna live. Maybe the Vax don't care about their hosts lasting that long, or am I gonna be pulling that elf shit and live for centuries? It's not like anyone fucking knows for sure.

James grunted and changed lanes. He pushed the

thought out of his mind. Worrying about how long he might live approached the most pointless thing he could do at that moment. Why worry about something he couldn't control? That was the essence of how someone made their life complicated.

"I had this truck before I met Shay," James muttered. "And I'm gonna spend the rest of my life with her."

There had been repairs throughout the years, but it wasn't like every piece of his truck had been replaced. The soul of the original vehicle remained—the essence of the machine that had helped save his life on countless jobs.

James' phone rang with a call from Heather. He sent it to speaker.

"You're supposed to be taking a few extra days off and spending them with your son," James answered. "Shay's got Peyton looking into all those addresses. You don't need to worry about that shit. I thought I made that clear."

"Where's Shay right now?" Heather asked, panic tingeing her voice.

James frowned. "At our house. Why?"

Heather took a deep breath. "You know I monitor for anything related to you, right? I've got a billion filters, spiders, and algorithms on it so I don't end up following up on a bunch of horny fangirls' erotic fiction where you run off to Mexico with them and crap like that, but I've got a lot of automated James Brownstone searching going on."

James grunted as he tried to process the onslaught of information. "Erotic fiction and Mexico? What the fuck?" He shook his head. "What's going on exactly? You saying you found something other than horny fangirls?"

"Yes, but I'm not sure what it is. There is a lot of weird

chatter on the net and certain encrypted radio bands. I dug into it a little more, and as best I can tell, the National Guard is being covertly mobilized all over California and routed toward Los Angeles County and Orange County. There are also some high-level communications with LAPD and a few other major police departments about some mysterious 'imminent emergency declaration.'"

James frowned. "What the hell? What's going on?"

Heather sighed. "That's it—I don't know. I can't find any clear explanation, and trust me, I've hacked some decently high-level systems to look for them. It's clear that the government's about to declare some sort of emergency in those counties, but that's not what's got me worried."

"What *has* got you worried?" James asked, his hands tightening on the wheel.

"I did find one line in a highly encrypted message to the commander of a National Guard unit being sent to LA. It was a lot of boilerplate about controlling looting and minimizing civilian injuries, but at the bottom..." Heather sucked in a breath. "It read, 'Per our previous communication, please be advised that personnel and assets assigned to your unit may be tasked to aid in the collection of the bounty hunter. The collection is necessary prior to the beginning of Operation Red Weed.'"

"What the fuck is 'Operation Red Weed?'" James asked.

"Red weed was a plant in Wells' *War of the Worlds*. That can't be a coincidence."

Fuck. Am I going to have to blow up a city now?

"They might not be talking about me," James suggested, but he didn't believe it even as he said the words. How many other alien bounty hunters were there in LA?

"Bullshit, they aren't. James, you need to collect Shay and get the hell out of LA. If they're sending the military after you and talking about alien invasion books, then they're not messing around. This is going to be worse than Fortis, because they might be sending the entire military after you."

James scoffed. "Fuck it. Fuck *them*. I'm not going anywhere."

"What?" Heather responded. "Are you listening to me? It's very likely that within the next few hours, the government may use military forces to lock down LA, and they might be doing that to take you down."

"I'm not running. No one will chase me out of my home. I've taken down too many fucking assholes and threats to this country to let any douchebags run me away from my hometown." James growled. "I'm not gonna beat down some poor National Guard sonofabitch if I don't have to, but I might have to cut up a few tanks or some shit to make my position clear. I bet you some politician wants to make a point."

"Probably, but who cares? That politician might be ready to throw some nasty stuff at you."

"If I run now, I'll never be able to stop running," James growled. "Where the fuck am I going to go? Argentina?"

James did a mirror check. There weren't any drones or suspicious vehicles following him. There certainly weren't any large military trucks. "Keep an eye out. I'm heading back home to get ready. I'll grab a receiver when I'm there. I'm making my fucking stand."

Shay slapped a magazine into a .45 pistol in James' basement. "Don't you have any 9mms? I prefer 9mms. Just something about them I like."

"You know I don't like 9mms." James shrugged and pulled off the spacer separating his amulet from his body. Pain spiked through his upper chest as the symbiont's tendrils spread.

Initiation, Whispy sent.

James looked at his emergency ass-kicking supplies. He didn't have much in the way of non-lethal weapons other than a small number of sonic grenades, and Shay had taken most of those.

Fuck. It's one thing to take down murderous bastards like Fortis, but I don't want to hurt some poor bastard who is just doing his duty. Fuck the government bastards starting trouble.

"James," Heather transmitted through his receiver. "You've got three government sedans heading your way."

"Any soldiers?" James asked.

"I'm seeing some military vehicles loading up elsewhere in the city, but there's nothing heading your way. Thermals indicate multiple people inside the sedans, but they don't look like they're carrying rifles, from what I can tell, and they aren't even fully loaded."

"Good. That means it's probably more Fortis assholes, or even Daniel and his friends. I don't have to feel bad about this." James grabbed a few extra magazines and stuck them in the pouches in his tactical vest. "I don't get this shit," he rumbled. "Why would they suddenly come at me now?"

"Who the fuck knows?" Shay asked. "But please tell me you're not planning to roll over and play nice? If the government locks you up, they might never let you out. They *know* how dangerous you are."

Engage and kill the enemy, Whispy demanded.

We'll see.

"I'm not going anywhere, and I'm not going to some CIA prison." James grabbed a few throwing knives and tucked them into sheaths, then jogged up the stairs with Shay trailing close behind.

They emerged from the basement to find Thomas wagging his tail and staring at them from right in front of the basement stairs. He barked and ran around in a circle.

"It's not playtime, boy." James pointed to the dog. "Take him downstairs, Shay. Get him some food and water and lock him in there. If they blow the rest of the house, the basement should survive. I made sure of that shit after the last time. If they take my ass out, you run. You can get your revenge later."

Shay frowned. "I should be out there with you."

James shook his head. "If they can take me out with Whispy on, your ring and pendant aren't gonna be enough." He took a deep breath. "Promise me."

Shay rolled her eyes. "I'll wait inside, but if they don't kill you right away, I'm joining in the fun. Okay?"

"Fair enough." James shrugged.

Shay grinned. "And be careful."

"Nope."

"Nope?" Shay raised an eyebrow.

James gave her a feral grin. "They're the ones who need to be careful."

Shay grinned back. "That's more like it. Remind those fuckers who you are."

Thomas barked again, and Shay shooed him downstairs.

James waited a few more seconds before marching over to his front door. He threw it open and stepped onto his porch. He stood and waited for the government vehicles to arrive, ignoring Whispy's increasingly strident calls for mayhem and death. A thousand years might pass, but the amulet would continue to offer the same advice: kill and grow stronger.

Three black dots down the street morphed into sedans with tinted windows. The vehicles didn't scream down the street, instead obeying the speed limit. No one fired a weapon or an artifact.

Two of the sedans pulled into the driveway, while the third parked along the curb. The back door to one driveway vehicles opened, and a familiar politician stepped out with a practiced smile on his face.

"Hello, son," Senator Johnston offered. "I'm sorry to show up unannounced and suddenly, but we've got a bit of a situation. I'm going to need you to come with me." His gaze focused on the various implements of death James carried. "I probably should have called ahead, but we knew you were here, and we didn't want to take the risk of tipping certain...people off."

James grunted. "You arresting me?"

"Arresting you?" Senator Johnston looked bemused. "Now why would I do that, son?"

No one else had stepped out of the vehicles.

"Any tactical drones coming, Heather?" James asked, keeping his voice low.

"Nothing nearby but a few traffic drones," Heather replied.

"Got someone else listening in, son?" Senator Johnston asked. "Miss Carson, perhaps? Or one of your little hacker friends?"

James glared at the other man. "Are you here to fucking arrest me or not?"

The confusion on the senator's face deepened. "Even if I wanted to arrest you, I don't even think that's possible, not without your cooperation. We both know that. I had my opportunity to get rid of you, and I chose to save you for reasons I definitely don't regret." He gestured to the vest. "You thought I was coming to arrest you?"

"Why is the National Guard mobilizing?" James barked.

Senator Johnston smiled but didn't answer.

James frowned and realized something important. "Heather, is it just the Guard mobilizing?" he murmured. "What about the rest of the military?"

"There's been a little unusual Air Force activity, but nothing local. Wait. Huh. That's weird." A flurry of intense typing sounded over the line.

"What's weird?" James murmured.

"Oh, one of my little spiders flagged something strange. If I understand what I'm reading correctly, the military is directly tasking a bunch of radio and optical telescopes all of a sudden," Heather explained. "I'm not quite sure what that's about. Meteor, maybe?"

James had a few ideas about what they might be looking for, but the old man standing in front of him held all the answers. "What's Operation Red Weed?"

"You know, even the average soldier about to carry it

out doesn't truly understand what it is. The name's a bit blatant, but sometimes the best way to hide something is right in the open. Everyone expects a lie, not the truth." Senator Johnston heaved a heavy sigh and closed his eyes for a moment. "I'm always telling everyone else to not underestimate you, but then here I go doing just that. You're not just a man with extraordinary physical gifts, you have extraordinary resources and loyal personnel."

"Get to the fucking point," James growled, flexing his fingers.

Senator Johnston lifted his hands in a calming gesture. "I'm asking you, son, on behalf of your country and planet, to lend us a helping hand."

"What, this is just some job shit?" James snorted. "Some assholes like the Council or something? If you've already sent guys at them and they've lost, I'll consider it, but I'm getting ready to semi-retire. I don't know if I want to face off against someone like the Council and cause trouble for myself down the line. I've got a wedding coming up."

"If only it were so simple." Senator Johnston shook his head. "This isn't about bounties, son, or even dangerous magical criminal groups."

"Then what the fuck *is* it about?"

Senator Johnston locked eyes with James. "One of your relatives is on the way, son, and he's already been disagreeable. We think it's best if you had a little talk with him."

ENGAGE AND KILL THE ENEMY, Whispy screamed in James' mind. *Achieve primary directive: destroy all Vax symbionts.*

Shut up. I need to concentrate.

James didn't realize he'd been growling for several

seconds. "They're here? Where?" Rage and anger flowed through him, the frustration of an entire life bubbling out.

Sufficient power for advanced transformation, Whispy reported.

Not yet.

"Not here," Senator Johnston replied. "Not yet. Oriceran. Lots of people have already died, son. I can't talk about it right now in detail, but we have good reason to believe that your relative is coming to Los Angeles, and we need your help."

James lowered his head and shook it. "Fine. Let me get Shay."

CHAPTER TWELVE

Tyler crossed his arms. He and Maria walked down the hallway from his office in the back of the Black Sun on their way to the main bar. The conversation they had shared both surprised and irritated the information broker.

I can't believe Brownstone would stab me in the back like this. It's one thing that he chose someone else, but he had to choose that smug drunken asshole Smite-Williams?

"Fine, I'll do it, but I'm a little pissed," Tyler muttered. "I still can't believe it, though."

Maria frowned. "Why are you pissed about Brownstone asking you to be a groomsman? It's not like I thought you would fall down delirious with happiness over being asked, but you seem like you're genuinely annoyed that he asked you. What gives?"

Tyler shook his head. "I'm not annoyed he asked me. I thought he was going to offer me something else, is all."

"What did you think he was going to offer you? A big pile of money?" Maria rolled her eyes. "I know you're greedy as hell, but that's not how this works. I mean, you've been to a wedding before. You know how this shit is supposed to go down."

"Yeah, yeah, I know." Tyler shook his head and stopped before they entered the crowded main bar room. "I just thought…" He would sound like an idiot if he said it aloud, but he'd backed himself into a corner.

Shit. I should have just kept my mouth shut and not acted so surprised.

"You thought what?" Maria asked, her face showing by bewilderment.

Tyler sighed and averted his eyes. "When you started talking, I thought you were going to say that Brownstone wanted me to be his best man. Understand my irritation now?"

Maria burst out laughing. She bent over, slapped her knee, and pointed at Tyler. "Seriously? You, Brownstone's best man? That's the funniest thing I've heard this month."

The info broker crossed his arms and frowned. "It's not *that* stupid or funny. You're Shay's maid of honor."

"Shay and I actually get along. Half the time you hate his ass and publicly rant about him." Maria shrugged. "I wasn't sure you would even agree to be a groomsman."

"Sure, I've got my complaints, but I've also worked with him. I provide him info, and I've shown my respect. You don't understand because you're a woman. Men are different." Tyler nodded with smug certitude in an attempt to cover his embarrassment.

"This ought to be good." Maria rolled her eyes. "Do enlighten me, oh King of Men. Why should you be his best man?"

Tyler slapped his chest. "You have to understand. Brownstone and me, we have a special relationship. It's built on mutual respect and challenge. We bring out the best in each other by pushing each other to our limits. It's why I'm rich now, and it's why Brownstone recognized I could help him with things like the pay-per-view."

Maria rolled her eyes. "Because that went so well." She waved a hand. "Sure, whatever you have to tell yourself to get to sleep at night. Anyways, Brownstone was rich before he met you, and, Tyler, what you're describing is being frenemies, which is more a chick thing than a guy thing in most situations."

"Just saying," Tyler grumbled. "It would have been nice."

A gang member turned the corner, heading toward the bathroom. His brow was furrowed, and he glanced at the front door. "Is some big shit happening, Tyler?"

Tyler frowned. "There's always shit happening, but you don't get to find out about it for free. You know that. I'm running a business here. You narrow the scope of the request down, and we'll talk about price. Then, and only then, do you get info. Unless you've got some info to trade me?"

The gang member shook his head. "Nah, man. I don't mean shit like that." He nodded at the door. "I just came in, and I saw some weird stuff outside."

"You better not just be in here to use the bathroom," Tyler replied, glaring at the man. "The bathrooms are for paying customers only. You better not think I won't know, and you better not be even thinking about doing drugs in there. Neutral ground doesn't mean anything goes."

Maria nodded her agreement, casting a stern gaze on the young gang member.

"Nah, bitch, just listen already." The gang member gestured toward the front door. "So I'm getting out of my car to come in, you know, and I'm seeing, like, all these Army trucks driving by. Soldiers full up with helmets and big-ass rifles like they're ready to go fuck up the Council or some shit. I looked at my phone, and it ain't saying shit about anything big going on, so why is G.I. Joe here?"

What the hell?

Despite Tyler's surprise, he kept a calm expression. He didn't want some low-level gang member seeing him disconcerted over learning something.

"That's interesting. Very interesting." Tyler looked at the tv, hoping there might be a clue there. "Since when the hell does this crowd like golf?" he asked.

"Maybe they know something." Maria pointed at two uniformed officers sitting at the bar.

Tyler, Maria, and the gangbanger walked over to the cops.

"Hey, Jeff," Maria greeted the older of the two cops.

"Hey, Maria," Jeff responded. "What's up?"

Maria glanced at the gang member and then back at Jeff. "You hear anything about anything going on? Anything that might involve the military? Coordinated level fives coming into the city or something?"

Jeff shrugged. "I haven't heard anything like that." He frowned. "Except…we did get a notice to be on standby for extra shifts, but no one seems to know why." He lifted his glass. It was filled with a dark liquid. "That's why this is just Coke rather than rum and Coke. Hey, I figure a little overtime never hurt the bank account."

Tyler surveyed the room, his stomach tightening. He didn't like to be behind when it came to useful information. "There's no way a bunch of level fives is about to show up without me hearing about it. Do you know how much money that kind of information would be worth to Brownstone?"

"I don't know what to tell you, Tyler." The cop shrugged, looking as confused as Tyler felt. "Maybe it's a surprise visit by the President or some Oriceran bigwig?" Jeff snapped. "What if King Oriceran himself is coming? That would be cool."

Maria snorted. "This is LA, not some warzone. Why would it need to be—"

Shrill alarms sounded from everyone's phone simultaneously, and the golf vanished from the television. A familiar harsh tone played from the television, the alert signal for the Emergency Broadcast System. Every man and woman looked up at the tv with bated breath.

The Seal of the Office of the President of the United States appeared with a large text overlay.

Stand by for an emergency message from the President of the United States of America.

"What the fuck?" Tyler whispered. He ran his hands through his hair. "What is going on?"

Maria swallowed. "The last time I saw one of these was when the Galbrathians blew up the Seattle kemana."

The President appeared. He sat behind his desk in the Oval Office with a concerned look on his face. Silence swept the Black Sun.

"My fellow Americans," the President began. "It brings me no pleasure to have to contact you in this way, but it will be important in the coming days that the people of this country come together to aid the greater Los Angeles area in their time of need. That is what is greatest about our country: how we hold out a hand for our neighbor when he's in trouble."

The gang member trembled. "What the fuck is he talking about? What's going on?"

"Shut the fuck up," Tyler snapped.

The man swallowed and nodded.

"Let me first provide some context," the President continued. He folded his hands in front of him. "Many people are familiar with the so-called Broken Arrow scenario, wherein the government loses control of a nuclear weapon."

Tyler's eyes widened, and concerned murmurs passed through the room.

Oh, fuck me with a rusty spoon. A nuke?

The President sighed. "But times have changed. It used to be that nuclear weapons represented the pinnacle of destruction on this planet. However, with the return of magic to Earth, other dangerous scenarios are now possible, including a scenario that wouldn't have been as much of a concern before the gates opened. The incident requiring this broadcast doesn't involve a Broken Arrow. It involves a Broken Wand."

Maria stumbled toward the bar and caught herself with one arm. "We're so fucked."

"A Broken Wand," the President explained, "is the official code for a lost MAMD: a magical artifact of mass destruction. I won't lie or mislead you. Large numbers of trained and skilled personnel from the military, the Paranormal Defense Agency, the Federal Bureau of Investigation, and the Department of Homeland Security, along with skilled magical personnel on loan from Oriceran, are in the process of being deployed to the greater Los Angeles area to recover this artifact. Those personnel will locate and disable this device if possible, but there is a non-negligible chance of activation and the subsequent destruction of the greater Los Angeles area."

Every criminal, cop, and tourist in the bar stared at the tv, their attention glued to President. Many were slack-jawed.

The President frowned. "Let me be clear: there is no terrorist threat at this time. This unfortunate incident has to do with a unique combination of events that is unlikely to ever occur again, but that doesn't change the fact that millions of American lives are at risk, and we need to employ extraordinary measures to protect those lives. Therefore, in coordination with the governor, a State of Emergency is hereby declared, along with martial law."

Several men shot from their seats. "What the fuck? Martial law?"

"That explains the soldiers," Tyler offered.

"As of now, and based on consultation with experts about the risk areas, Los Angeles and Orange Counties are hereby under a mandatory evacuation order," the President declared. "The National Guard is being deployed to perform block-by-block sweeps and help with the evacuation. Military transport vehicles and aircraft will be helping to facilitate the evacuation. If you can get to a major airport without blocking the roads, please do so. You will be flown to a safe location out of the potential influence zone of the MAMD. In addition, portals are being established in key locations throughout the region." Several web addresses appeared on the bottom of the screen. "Visit any of these sites for a complete list of nearby locations, but I can already inform you that the Oriceran Consulate portals will take people to Sacramento, San Francisco, and San Diego. DHS and FEMA agents in those areas will provide temporary shelter for evacuees."

Tyler rubbed his temples. "This shit isn't happening. No fucking way is this shit happening."

Maria swallowed, her face pale. "We trained for this scenario in the AET, but it's something I hoped to never see in my own city."

The President's expression hardened. "There are always those who will seek to take advantage of situations in times of trouble. While I encourage everyone to leave until such time as the evacuation order is rescinded, note that military patrols will be protecting the city at great risk to themselves until a full evacuation of all civilians is achieved. The governor has made it clear, with the support of the federal government and the White House, that there will be zero tolerance for looters or criminal activity. What we are about to attempt is dangerous, but the risk of millions of lives means it's more dangerous not to leave. May God have mercy on us all in this dark time, and with any luck, you will all be able to return to your homes soon. Good luck, and God bless."

The Presidential seal replaced the man.

Half the bar fled toward the door, shouting, the young

gang member first among them. A waitress dropped a tray filled with drinks and ran out the door. Others trampled over the shattered glass. Under normal circumstances, Tyler would be furious, but he barely registered his fleeing employees or all the customers skipping out on payment.

Tyler scrubbed a hand over his face. "Well, fuck. I didn't see that coming—and I see everything coming—but it makes sense. If it's not terrorists or criminals but just a government fuck-up, nothing would have leaked to the streets."

Maria took a few deep breaths and straightened her back. "Maybe this is something Brownstone can help with."

Tyler let out a strangled laugh. "How? You heard the President. The government is searching for the artifact. This isn't something that can be solved by punching someone really hard. Even Brownstone will need to evacuate. I doubt he can survive an explosion big enough to blow up a city."

Jeff and the other police officer at the bar frowned down at their phones. "We've got to go."

Maria nodded. "Good luck, guys."

Darkness flavored the cop's chuckle. "I don't think anyone in this city can say they have good luck now." He hopped off his stool and joined the stream of customers fleeing the Black Sun.

"We need to get the hell out, too," Tyler declared. "I'm not happy to have to leave, but I've got plenty of cash in hidden accounts. Even if this entire country becomes a crater, I can come back from it. I say we hit the Oriceran Consulate and take a portal to San Diego. There will be fewer people taking the portals because they're afraid of magic."

"I…" Maria shook her head. "I'm not sure. I need to call Brownstone and figure out what the agency is going to do."

"What? Fuck Brownstone! I know he's your boss, but he doesn't outrank the fucking President!" Tyler threw up his arms. "We need to get the hell out of here. Not only that, we *have* to get the hell out of here. We're under mandatory evacuation and martial law. I'm not going to get in a fight with some soldier over you worrying about Brownstone."

People continued rushing out the front.

"Fine." Maria grimaced and looked at the front door. "Let's just swing by my place before the damned National Guard locks down the entire city. If Los Angeles is about to become a crater, I want to make sure I have a few keepsakes."

CHAPTER THIRTEEN

J ames had to admit that the seats in the government car were damned comfortable. A truck filled with soldiers zoomed past. He had unbonded Whispy before Senator Johnston explained what had happened on Oriceran. A symbiont screeching in his mind for battle against another Vax was distracting.

"You're lying to the entire country," James commented. "Everyone thinks you lost a magical nuke."

"True enough, but a lot of people lied to the entire world about magic for much longer. We're lying to protect people." Senator Johnston nodded. "I know it sounds self-serving, but it's for their own good. If the Vax comes here, a lot of people might die, so the best thing to do is to get everyone out of the way. Simple as that, really."

Shay scoffed from the other side of James. "And it's not about cutting down on the number of witnesses? A few statements here and there to the soldiers and remaining cops and it's easy to keep them quiet, but you get millions of phones with cameras uploading instantly to the net, it'll be too many questions you have to answer. The truth about aliens will come out."

"Controlling the information certainly figures into it. I'm not going to deny that," Senator Johnston replied. "While a little technology and magic can go a long way toward keeping curious eyes off the situation, particularly satellites, the fewer people actually in the city, the easier it'll be."

"But you can't even be sure the Vax will come over." Shay let out a dark chuckle. "You might be evacuating the entire area for nothing."

"Then it'll be a nice training exercise for everyone involved, but this is definitely one time I would like to err on the side of caution rather than hoping it all turns out all right. If we had better luck, the Vax wouldn't have shown on this planet for a few hundred years. We would have had time to develop better ray guns and spells."

James grunted and shook his head. He uncurled his fists, which he didn't even remember clenching. "The asshole will come. I guarantee it. There's no fucking way this is a big coincidence, especially since Corey is freaking out and saying it's not normal, according to what you've told me. The Vax asshole might have blown up an Oriceran town, but he's here for me." He chuckled.

The senator raised an eyebrow. "You find this funny, son? It's good to not let a situation overwhelm you, but I'm a little surprised."

"Nah, it's not funny. Not really." James shrugged. "Okay, kind of funny. I just was thinking about how Shay was saying that if anything fucked up the wedding, I'd better blow up a city in revenge. Looks like that might happen, but I'll make sure I take that fucker with it."

Shay elbowed James. "If you win the fight, it'll be fine. The island I'm going to rent is off the coast of Southern California, sure, but it's far enough away from Los Angeles that it shouldn't be affected."

Senator Johnston glanced at them, an amused look on his face. "We'd prefer it if you stopped the Vax, but, yes, we are prepared for collateral damage, and we do understand that it's inevitable the city will take damage." He pulled out his phone and tapped in a few commands. "A limited amount of damage might even be easily repairable with magic if we need to conceal certain realities, but our primary concern is taking the bastard out."

"You don't need the Oricerans to get to Oriceran," Shay observed. "We could just send James over there anyway and let him do his thing. You said the Purifier isn't near any cities right now."

Senator Johnston shook his head. "When this is all over, we don't want to be on the brink of war with the Oricerans. We'll handle this here. It'll show the Oricerans that Earth can defend itself. Hell, it'll show that the United States can defend the Earth by ourselves. If you want peace, prepare for war, and one way to do that is show strength."

"You think Oriceran is going to attack the Earth?" Doubt filled Shay's voice.

"I think that you never know what's going to happen. Earth history, let alone the return of magic, proves that well enough, and I believe it's a good idea to plan for the future so you don't get blindsided by it."

"Where we going right now?" James asked.

"Los Angeles Air Force Base. Not much in the way of fancy planes there, but it is where the Space and Missile Systems Center is, so it's a nice place to help coordinate the response." Senator Johnston swiped on his phone. "I'm ultimately calling the shots on this little party. It's the best of both worlds. If I do well, no one gets hurt, and no one even knows I was involved, but if it goes south, then I'm the scapegoat they hang for the loss of Los Angeles." He offered a toothy grin to James. "A politician who actually has to take responsibility. Scary thought, isn't it?"

"Why are you even here?" James nodded to the senator's phone. "You could sit your ass in DC and do everything over a computer or phone."

"Because if something bad goes down and we're not able to finish evacuation before your relative arrives, I think it's important for a few high-up people to have skin in the game. A lot of innocent people might still end up at risk, not to mention all the military personnel we're asking to stick around." Senator Johnston shrugged. "I'm not the President. The country can continue on just fine if my old ass dies."

James grunted. "I can respect that."

"Besides, being at the heart of this place will help us coordinate easier with some other bases involved in the control of space assets."

"Space assets? Why does that matter? The Vax don't travel through space. They portal."

Senator Johnston held up his phone. There was a blurry picture of a long, narrow gray shape. He swiped, and there was another blurry picture. Two more swipes, same thing. A final swipe revealed four dots in the expanse of space.

Shay leaned forward, her eyes narrowed. "What are these? Asteroids? Comets?"

Senator Johnston lowered his phone and shook his head. "Imagery analysis indicates they are four smooth and very large and narrow objects with a number of hard angles and unusual reflectivity, and they are much hotter on one end. There are all sorts of other fancy things they can detect using fancy instruments, but there is only so much they can do with space telescopes, and not much they can do with magic so far away. These objects are still halfway across the Solar System, but they're on their way to Earth, and they're traveling damned fast."

"Ships," Shay offered. "Those are ships."

James sighed. If the Vax didn't use ships, that left only one obvious possibility. He'd already worried about this possibility when Heather mentioned the strange tasking of the telescopes by the military. "It's an Alliance fleet."

"That's what we're assuming," Senator Johnston replied. "The Alliance representative already threatened to handle the situation without our permission. This is proof that they aren't content to let us solve this little problem ourselves. Given what they've said previously, I would also guess these aren't cruise ships filled with alien tourists. They threatened to bombard you with anti-matter torpedoes from a much smaller ship, so they must have a lot of fancy weapons on these bigger ships. Not only that, they're paranoid enough to bring four when one might have been enough."

Shay leaned back, her eyes flicking to the side as several

motorcycles zoomed past the car going the opposite direction. "Can the Vax take out ships in orbit?"

"Who knows? The Alliance is remarkably unwilling to share concrete intelligence on the matter. I think they figure if we know too much, we won't accept their help."

James growled. "It doesn't matter. You're saying they're going to attack."

"I'm saying there's a good of chance of that, yes." Senator Johnston replied. "If the Vax comes to LA, I presume the Alliance would bombard it, and I'm not convinced they'll stop if we haven't finished the evacuation."

James furrowed his brow. "I can't fucking fly. Not even sure if Whispy works in space. How the fuck am I supposed to stop four spaceships?"

Senator Johnston waved a hand. "You don't need to worry about it, son. We've already got a plan for that. It's a little something I've been working on for a while. It uses our advantages and their disadvantages. It'll also help send a message that our backward little planet can bite when necessary." Johnston grinned, reminding James a little of a soberer Professor. "You only need to concentrate on your relative, because we're not going to be stupid about this. This isn't going to be like some alien invasion movie where we send a bunch of cannon-fodder soldiers to die pointlessly against an enemy we know is beyond them." He clucked his tongue. "It's always the same. Step one, send military personnel to die. Step two, drop a nuke. Step three, realize the nuke didn't work. Step four, hope and pray you find a weakness. We're going to skip past step four and send you."

Shay cleared her throat. "James is tough, and he has been exposed to radiation, thermal energy, and that kind of thing, but I'm not sure he would survive a nuke. I get the Oricerans refuse to break the Great Treaty, but what about nuking the guy when he comes over?"

"We're not evacuating Los Angeles for fun, Miss Carson, and we have every reason to believe he'll appear in Los Angeles. We're evacuating the city to minimize the loss of life, and we're hoping that James here can do his best to take out the Vax bastard and minimize the overall damage to the city." Senator Johnston pointed over his shoulder with his thumb at a passing gas station. "We drop a nuke, and even if we win, we've lost. We will have just taken out one of the major cities in the United States, and it only gets worse. My people tell me if that Vax arrives in the next few days, there's no way in hell we'll have this city totally evacuated. Best-case scenario, even excluding military personnel, we're still talking thousands of people." Any hint of humor or light-heartedness left the senator's face. "With God as my witness right here, Miss Carson, I will do everything I can to prevent the deaths of thousands of Americans up to and including sacrificing my own life."

Shay blinked and nodded. Death and destruction were one thing, but the potential scale of the casualties went well beyond the kind of pain James and Shay had delivered even to the Nuevo Gulf Cartel, and those bastards had had it coming.

James stared straight ahead, the movement of the cars in both lanes idly drawing his attention as he thought about everything he had been told. He had always assumed the Vax would come, but for some reason, he had allowed himself to believe it would be years in the future, or maybe decades.

If I want a peaceful life, I'm gonna have to fight for it. It's time for a fucking galactic Brownstone Effect.

Senator Johnston handed James his phone. "Sorry, son. The minute you got in this car, we started jamming your phone and your hacker friend. We couldn't take the chance some Alliance assassin decided to take you out, but I'm sure you'll want to contact your daughter. Keep her at that school. She's far safer there than she'll be here, and I'm sure you have a few other calls you need to make."

James grunted. "Yeah. I've got one other thing I need from you for this shit."

"What's that?"

"I need someone to go pick up my dog," James explained. "And he better be well-fucking-treated, because if he isn't, the Purifier will look like a Cub Scout compared to me."

CHAPTER FOURTEEN

I kept wishing for Dad to quit bounty hunting, Alison thought, *but that wouldn't have made a difference this time.*

Alison swallowed when James finished explaining the situation. She clutched the handset of Headmistress Berens' phone in her hand. She had wondered why the headmistress had summoned her, but hadn't expected the news she had received.

The girl's stomach churned as she leaned forward in her chair over the front of the desk. While this wasn't the first time she had received an emergency call at school, it had never been in conjunction with the government declaring martial law and a state of emergency. Even when her father had fought the Council, it still felt like him doing what he always did: being a bounty hunter.

This felt different, like a soldier calling his daughter from the front lines.

"Alison, are you all right?" Headmistress Berens asked, concern on her face.

"Yeah, just taking in the news from my dad."

"I would like to tell you more," James rumbled over the phone, "but there's no point, and I don't have a huge amount of time right now. I just figured you should know the truth."

Alison would have preferred it if her father had called her directly. Having to process all her emotions in front of the headmistress of her school was uncomfortable.

Unfortunately, Alison didn't have any choice. Her father's attempts to call her on her phone had failed, and he'd called the headmistress in a last-minute act of desperation.

Alison wasn't surprised. They had experienced difficulties in recent weeks speaking with each other over her phone. The professors at the school were always adjusting the wards and other spells around the main building and the grounds. That was likely the reason.

The Entrepreneurs Club had even been complaining about it, since some of the recent modifications were disrupting a few of their research projects. She could easily imagine a time in the future where cell phones might not work at all on campus.

We'd really be separate from the world then.

"Dad," Alison whispered, "I should be there."

"No way," James rumbled back. "It makes no sense for you to be here. At least I know if you're back there at that school, you're safe, no matter what happens here. Besides, I'm not gonna lose. You know me. The closer I get to losing, the more pissed-off I get. I just figured you should know. I've got to go now. The senator's got to talk to me about other crap. You know how saving the world is. Lots of annoying details."

"Okay." Alison teared up. "I love you, Dad."

"Don't cry," James replied softly. "I can hear you choking up. Remember, it's just a few months until the wedding. I need you to keep it together until then."

"I… I will. You promise we'll have the wedding on time, right?"

"If we don't, your mom's gonna be a lot scarier than some assholes from space." James grunted. "I love you. Talk to you soon."

The call ended.

Alison barely noticed the headmistress as she handed back the handset. Feelings swirled inside and threatened to overwhelm her.

It hadn't been all that long ago when her dad had admitted he was an alien. As in all things, he had been blunt and straightforward during the conversation. Somehow learning he was an alien made sense. She couldn't even claim she was that surprised.

He's an alien, and I was a secret Drow princess. That's just the way things work in our family.

The truth didn't bother Alison for another reason. James Brownstone was her adopted father, so the revelation didn't change anything about her past. In addition, she had peered into his soul and knew he was a good person.

Alison attended a school with teachers from both Earth and Oriceran. All her dad telling her about being a Vax accomplished was adding a third planet to the list of places where people she loved had been born.

Learning about the rest of the Vax disturbed her. She couldn't help but compare her dad's situation to her own. The Drow had hunted for her, and they had killed to get to her. Even if the Drow weren't inherently evil, they'd done a lot of evil in the name of her people, just like the Vax.

Alison took a deep breath and turned her head slowly to look at Headmistress Berens. "Let me go. I want to take the train to LA. I need to be there. It feels wrong to sit here safe in Virginia when my dad's in danger."

Alison wasn't even sure what her father had told the headmistress. He'd only mentioned that she didn't know the total truth, and it was best if Alison didn't pass it along.

"Please, Headmistress," Alison added.

The dark-haired older woman sighed and shook her head. "Alison, your home is under a mandatory evacuation order. While I understand that your father is involved in this incident somehow, there's no way, as an educator and a person who cares about your well-being, that I'm sending you to a city with such a dangerous artifact. It's insane."

I should tell her the truth. I should tell her there is no artifact, and it's just my dad fighting another alien, but it's not like that's any better.

I could sneak out.

Headmistress Berens' gaze turned penetrating. "Within the next hour or so, I suspect every student on this campus will be worried about relatives or friends in California, but the best thing everyone can do right now is not create additional trouble. Do you understand?"

Alison's shoulders slumped. "But I feel so helpless."

"I understand that feeling all too well." The headmistress reached over to pat Alison's hand. "Believe in your father, and believe he will be all right. He's an unusual and impressive man, and I'm sure that however he's involved in this Broken Wand incident, he'll be a help."

Alison took a deep breath and nodded, then squared her shoulders and wiped away her tears. "You're right. My dad is not just anyone. He's the Granite Ghost, and he'll do what he can to make sure everyone's safe."

"I'm glad to hear you feel that way, Alison. I think the best thing to do in situations like this is simply go about your daily routine to get your mind off your problems."

"Thanks, Headmistress." Alison stood and pushed her chair back into place. "I'm going to do just that. I hope..." She shook her head, her face gleaming with pride. "I *know* my dad will be okay."

Shay tapped her fingers on her leg, waiting for Peyton to pick up.

He's smart. He wouldn't stick around.

"Hello?" Peyton answered, uncertainty in his voice.

Shay glanced at James and Senator Johnston, who were chatting quietly about potential strategies. Peyton's system had probably flagged the phone as a government device.

"It's not Fortis or shit like that," Shay explained. "It's me. I'm in a government car, not a prisoner or anything like that. They needed James' help, and I came along for the ride."

Peyton let out a sigh of relief. "It's hard not to be paranoid with all the craziness that's happening. I tried to call you right after the big alert went out, but I couldn't get hold of you, and then I didn't know what the hell was going on. Everything about this Broken Wand declaration smells like crap to me, but I also don't get why the government would do something so flashy, and why they might go after you. And thanks for the last cryptic message, by the way. Loved that. 'They might be coming for James. Things about to get bloody.'"

Shay furrowed her brow in consternation. "Okay, I'm not gonna call you a dumbass, but you really need to get the hell out of town."

"Shit. There is an actual MAMD?" Peyton groaned. "Just lay it out for me, because as bad as I hate to admit it. I'm totally lost right now."

Shay sighed. "It's not a MAMD, it's an AMD."

"Artifact of mass destruction?" Peyton asked. "What's the difference?"

"Not an artifact, an alien."

Shay proceeded to explain the situation succinctly.

"Well, fuck," Peyton muttered. "So even if James wins, there are probably going to be a lot of destroyed buildings. Hope that Vax doesn't portal in near my apartment or Warehouse Two."

"Can we try to keep a little perspective?" Shay asked. "And James *will* win."

Peyton scoffed. "In that case, all the more reason to hope that neither my apartment nor the warehouse gets blown up."

"Since when do you care so much about the warehouse?"

"I don't think you get how in tune I am with that pizza oven." Peyton let out a labored and melodramatic sigh. "I'm not sure I can produce the best pizza ever without it."

Shay rolled her eyes. She knew humor was Peyton's way of coping with stress, but she might have to slap him later anyway. "Just grab your cat and your girlfriend, if she hasn't left already, and run through a portal or take a plane or whatever you need to get way the hell away from here. James already called Heather, and she's on her way to the Oriceran Consulate with her son. Everybody at the agency has been ordered to retreat to Las Vegas until James says otherwise."

Peyton fell silent for a few long seconds. "This is the real deal, isn't it?"

"Yeah. It is, but I believe in him. I know he won't lose, not to some asshole who wasn't even smart enough to show up at the right address before he threw the first punch."

Peyton sighed. "I know you'll probably throat-punch me the next time you see me if I say what I'm thinking."

"Then think about what you're going to say carefully." Shay narrowed her eyes and checked on James again. He was still murmuring to Senator Johnston.

"Screw it. I'm just going to come out and say it. What about you? Why are you staying? You're the toughest woman I know, but even with your sword and all your artifacts, this isn't a fight you can help with. If even the military is deferring to James, you should too, and let's be honest: he could lose."

Shay ground her teeth. "He won't lose."

"I didn't say he *would* lose, I said he *could* lose. This is another Vax; another badass with a symbiont. It could end up anything from James curb-stomps the bastard to the Purifier tears him apart, and if that happens, you shouldn't be anywhere near that city. Because the only thing scarier than James Brownstone is a monster who beat him."

"I'm not leaving," Shay muttered.

"But it's not like you're going to help him fi—"

"I'm not leaving," Shay shouted.

James and Senator Johnston looked her way.

Shay locked eyes with James. "He needs to know that I believe he'll win, Peyton. He needs to know that I'll be waiting for him."

James gave her a tight nod.

Peyton groaned. "Fine. It's not like anyone can ever talk you out of doing anything you're determined to do. I'll have my phone. Assuming LA doesn't end up a radioactive crater, you know how to get hold of me. This will just be a little unscheduled vacation."

Shay managed a small grin. "Yeah. And secretly convince your girlfriend to get her pals to invent an anti-Vax-portal device. Who cares about all this talking to aliens and probes and shit?"

Peyton snorted. "If I'm going on vacation, I'm having a good time. No work, no talk about aliens or LA. Because one thing I've learned from everything that has happened in the last few years is that no matter how hard we plan, we're never truly in control. Good luck, Shay. Tell James to throw a few punches for me."

"I'll do that. And just to be clear, no matter what happens, we're having that damned wedding if I have to come back as a ghost."

Peyton laughed. "I'll keep that in mind."

CHAPTER FIFTEEN

Senator Johnston smiled and opened the door to the modest barracks room. Two twin beds were inside, along with two wooden desks and a small closet. A tv hung on the wall. "I know it's not luxury, but at least it's somewhere to stay."

Shay frowned as she stepped in after James. "If we just needed somewhere to sleep, we could have done that at our house."

James grunted and nodded his agreement.

"The problem is that the situation is still fluid," Senator Johnston replied. "We don't want to go looking for you at your home instead of just sending you in a helicopter or one of those fancy new dropships to wherever our boy pops out."

Shay rolled her eyes. "And we can't have our phones?"

"I mean, if Mr. Brownstone objects, it's not like we're in a position to fight him, but there's a strong possibility that the Alliance might decide to pull something even before their fleet arrives, which is why I'm having your phones driven around at random right now." The senator shrugged.

James marched over and laid down on the stiff bed, his hands beneath his head. "They want me to fight the Vax, but they don't even give me a decent bed? That's the government for you." He chuckled.

"So, in the car, you mentioned the Vax is marching to some resonance zone that might be where James crossed over?" Shay stated.

Senator Johnston closed the door and reached into his pocket. Something clicked inside, and he pulled his hand out. "Just making the room a little more secure to talk in, but yes, Miss Carson. That is the latest information, based on what the Oricerans have passed along to us. At his current pace, he will arrive in four days."

"Four days?" Shay scoffed. "And you rushed us over here now?"

"Four days isn't a lot of time. Even with the portals, we might not be able to evacuate the city."

"I understand, but we don't need to sit around for almost a week on our thumbs." Shay turned one of the desk chairs around and dropped into it, then crossed her arms and frowned. "And he hasn't attacked anywhere else?"

"There have been a few unfortunate encounters with small groups despite the best efforts of the Oricerans, but no villages or towns have been attacked."

James sat up. "If they know where he's going, they can set up a trap for him."

A slightly annoyed look passed over Senator Johnston's face. "You would think so, but that, unfortunately, doesn't seem to be what's going to happen. They are more than content to let him come over here and have us deal with him, but to be fair, it's not like they haven't tried. The truth is, they just don't have the personnel to deal with this problem, but we do. We have you." He reached into his pocket and pulled out two phones. He handed one to each of them. "I've got all the important numbers preprogrammed in there, including the people who will be bringing you your meals." He nodded at the tv. "Plenty of channels, including barbeque shows and whatnot, and we can get whatever books you might need."

"We're just supposed to wait in here?" Shay asked.

"That would be optimal. Not saying you can't walk around, but we ask that you not leave the base, and it's not exactly a tourist stop. I'll have some people go over to your house to grab some more clothes for you soon."

"It's fine," James rumbled. "Not like I'm gonna be able to concentrate on a bunch of other shit in the meantime. What about my dog?"

"I've got an intern taking him to San Diego. Don't worry, the intern's sole job is taking care of your dog." Senator Johnston opened the door. "Your planet thanks you for your assistance, Mr. Brownstone. Your country thanks you, and I personally thank you." He exited and closed the door behind him.

Shay furrowed her brow. "Shit. I'm trying to think of a way I can get to my warehouses to get my gear without the government being all up my ass. I don't care if this a War of the Worlds, I don't trust them knowing my places."

James grinned. "How do you know they don't already know?"

"I can still hide when I want to, but I'm not going to be much use if I don't have at least the *Masamune*."

James' grin faded. "This is one fight I don't want you involved in. This isn't like the government or some of the weird-ass monsters you fight on tomb raids. You've seen what I can do, and this asshole is supposed to be a tougher version of me."

Shay's face tightened, and she looked away. "I figured you were going to say that, and Peyton was trying to get me to straight-up run. I've been sitting here trying to come up with all the reasons it's bullshit."

"And what have you come up with?"

Shay shrugged. "Nothing. Unless I kill the Purifier with my first attack, he'll adapt, and for all we know, all the magic the Oricerans have thrown at him has made him immune to any magical weapons or artifacts I might bring."

James reached underneath his shirt and pulled out his amulet. He ran a finger over the inlaid crystals. "It's all gonna come to how well I use this."

"You think you can win?"

"I think Whispy and I have learned a lot of tricks these last few years, tricks some new bastard fresh from halfway across the galaxy won't have come up against." James chuckled. "Fucker won't know what hit him." His smile grew, and his heart rate sped up.

Shay stared at him and shook her head. "Is this the pay-per-view all over again?"

"What do you mean?"

"You almost seem like you're looking forward to it."

James tucked his amulet back under his shirt. "Maybe

Whispy's not the only one who wants to see how far I can go, but yeah, I'm looking forward to it. This shit has been hanging over me my entire life, and after I got those memories back, I knew this day would come. I'd rather just get it over with now when I can still do something about it than sixty years from now when I might have to bring a walker to the fight."

Shay stood and walked over to sit on the side of the bed next to James. "Do you ever question if you'll win? Not just now. Ever?"

James frowned as he thought that over. "Sometimes, but not often. When I was fighting those Drow, I thought I might lose. Thought about using the wish even, but the Clown of Doom took care of them. Now I don't really worry. If it's my time, it's my time. Until then, I'm going to beat down any assholes who deserve it and any fuckers who threaten the people I care about, and threatening my planet is threatening the people I care about."

Shay smiled. "Well, there's nothing to do but wait." A wicked grin followed. "I can think of something we can do to pass the time."

"What?"

Shay winked. "Practice for our honeymoon."

Trey paced back and forth in his living room, looking at his phone. "This is some crazy shit. Almost everyone from the agency has checked in with either me or Maria. Only a few people who haven't, a few of the newer guys, but they're on their way. A few of them ended up taking the portals. Got a few in Sacramento, and the rest in San Francisco."

Zoe offered him a languid smile from her chair as she caressed the fronds of a glowing orange plant in a pot. It brightened at her touch. "I'm sure it'll be fine."

Living with the witch had gotten Trey used to all sorts of weird magical plants. He just thought of them as stationary strange-looking dogs, and it made everything easier.

"*Fine?*" Trey asked. "Some crazy-ass magical nuke might go off in Los Angeles, and it'll be fine? Damn, girl, you and I have very different definitions of what 'fine' is."

Zoe lifted her hands and rested them in her lap. "I was watching the news. An unexpected number of people elected to use the portals, and not just the ones at the Consulate. They had to bring in more magicals to support them and handle the flow of foot traffic. The evacuation is proceeding even better than they planned. There's a lot of chaos in the destination cities, but at least people are getting out of Los Angeles."

Trey's phone buzzed and he looked at the message, disappointed when it was another bounty hunter checking in. "Damn it. I can't believe Nana turned off her phone at a time like this."

"Your aunt is handling it, right? Don't worry."

"You're right. Ain't nothing to do but wait. You're not gonna have a problem with Nana and Auntie Charlyce staying with us for a while, are you?"

Zoe shook her head. "No. I find your relatives pleasant and full of life."

Trey snorted. "Yeah, that's one way to describe them."

A few hours later, Trey checked his phone from his recliner. Zoe had already gone to bed. Every agency employee was now accounted for, with two notable exceptions: James and Charlyce.

The big man had made it clear he was helping with the situation in LA. Trey didn't understand why and how he was doing that, but he figured James would let him know all the details once the crisis was over.

That left Charlyce and, by extension, Trey's grandmother.

Trey frowned as he stared down at his phone. His aunt had told him she wouldn't call him until she and Nana Garfield were safe in Vegas since she knew he would be busy dealing with all the check-ins from the other agency employees.

If I call her now, it might be insulting and shit, but this ain't exactly a normal situation.

Trey raised his phone to dial, but just as he did, it came to life with a call from Charlyce.

Maybe I've got me some psychic powers.

Trey grinned and answered the phone. "Yo, Auntie Charlyce! You get stuck on the road or something? I've been up waiting for you and Nana. I'm getting tired."

"I can't find her!" Charlyce wailed.

CHAPTER SIXTEEN

"Huh?" Trey asked. "What are you talking about? What do you mean you can't find Nana?"

"She called me," Charlyce explained. "She told me she had to go grab some things and then check on someone else from church. She said she was going to evacuate on one of the soldier buses because the roads were too crowded, and I couldn't get to her anyway without getting stuck. She told me she would call me once she got on the bus, but she never called." She sighed. "So I went to go check her house. The traffic was bad, but she wasn't there. They had those numbers in the window like they were talking about on the news for the people counts, but the numbers showed she was gone when the soldiers came. I tried calling her, but her phone keeps going to voicemail."

Trey took a deep breath and slowly let it out. His heart pounded. He wasn't going to yell at his aunt in the middle of a massive counties-wide evacuation, but he needed a few things clarified. An old woman shouldn't be wandering LA in all the chaos.

Wait one damned second.

Trey's grandmother's words floated into his thoughts.

No, I want to die in this house.

"Damn it. I think she's still in LA," Trey explained. "I can't believe this. Of all the times to pull some stubborn stunt!"

"I don't understand. What should I do?"

"Where are you right now?" Trey asked. "And can you drive?"

Charlyce sighed. "The roads are still pretty jammed up."

"Then go find the National Guard or go to one of the portals," Trey suggested. "Get out of there as soon as possible."

There was no way in hell he would risk losing two relatives.

"I can't just leave her," Charlyce complained. "What if something happens? What if the thing blows up?"

Trey sighed. "Don't worry. I'll handle finding her. Remember who my girlfriend is. She's got a way of finding things and people. It ain't like Nana knows counter-magic shit, even if she's hiding out."

"I'm sorry, Trey. I should have gone straight to pick her up like you told me."

"It ain't your fault. She tricked you." Trey stood and frowned. "I told you how she was complaining about not wanting to move, but I ain't letting her get hurt, even if I have to drag her back. You just get out of LA and leave everything else to me. I'm a bounty hunter. I can find one old woman."

Senator Johnston swirled the ice cubes in his glass of whiskey. Drinking while staring down a dangerous alien attack might not be all that professional, but so far Operations Red Weed and Dandelion were both proceeding better than he could have hoped. After decades of service in the government, that was a rare occurrence.

Brownstone was on board with their plan to engage the Vax, and if the Purifier kept to his current pace, they might actually have a shot of the city being empty if he even bothered to come over to LA. Even though the senator believed the Vax would travel to Earth, he held out a small hope that he wouldn't.

It'd be funny if the Purifier walked all that way and disappeared at the end of this back to the hell planet he came from.

Senator Johnston lifted the glass to his lips and took a sip. They'd set him up in an empty office near the base commander's. The accommodations were more spartan than he was used to, not that it mattered. He was spending most of his time in conference rooms or on the move making calls. If the government needed their next plan, Operation Gulliver, he wouldn't even be staying on base.

Skin in the game. That's what I keep telling myself—skin in the game. Maybe if I say it enough, I'll actually believe it, and not feel like the world's greatest fool for sitting at Ground Zero of an alien invasion.

Senator Johnston's desk phone rang. The Caller ID was a bearer of bad news. He picked it up and sighed.

"Hello, Corey," Senator Johnston answered.

"The line is now secure on my end," the alien replied.

"Are we going to have another tiresome discussion?

We're handling this our way, and we don't rightly care what the Alliance thinks about it."

Corey chuckled. "So far, we think you've done an excellent job of handling things."

"Is that so?" Senator Johnston replied.

"If anything, I'm glad you're being efficient in your evacuation of Los Angeles. You've made a difficult decision far easier, and I wanted to thank you for that. It makes what has to happen next that much easier."

The senator shot up, his heart racing. He didn't like how confident the Shepherd sounded. They already had one overconfident alien on his way to cause trouble. They didn't need another.

"Given how much danger the Purifier represents, it wasn't like we were going to leave millions of potential victims in his path," Senator Johnston replied. "Just because we don't agree with the Alliance about handling the situation doesn't mean we don't take what you've said about the Vax seriously."

"Again, that's good to hear." Any hint of mirth left Corey's voice. "I'm calling because what we have to do next is dangerous, and it will fundamentally change the relationship between the Alliance and Earth. However, after consulting my superiors, we've decided that since you can't stop it anyway, it's better if we tell you. That way you can withdraw any residual forces from the LA area before it's too late, and we can avoid unnecessary casualties."

"What are you talking about, my alien friend?" Senator Johnston's voice revealed his thinly veiled anger. "Because if you're talking about what I think you're talking about, we're going to have to go beyond agreeing to disagree."

"I know you've detected the incoming fleet," Corey replied. "I should let you know that your telescope facilities have poor security, even by human standards. You might want to change that situation if you're going to use them to track alien space fleets."

Senator Johnston chuckled. "I won't insult you by pretending not to know what you're talking about. Yes, we're aware of your little fleet, but like you said, it's not like we're in a position to do much about it *at this moment.*"

"I'm glad you're being reasonable about this. None of us are happy about what must be done, but it's the best for both Earth and the Alliance in the long run."

Senator Johnston took a deep breath. The decisions made in the next few minutes could have ramifications for decades, if not centuries. "If you're calling to beg forgiveness, you should at least explain exactly what you plan to do."

A tense silence passed between them.

"The Vax are powerful, but they're not immortal, even when they're fully adapted," Corey finally explained. "They can be surprisingly resilient against many weapons, but the reality is they are still individual hosts connected to an advanced but not godlike technology. The application of a sufficient amount of destructive power can end them, even if they're adapted to it. The important thing is to ensure there is nothing left for regeneration. You'd be surprised how easily a fully prepared Vax can reconstitute itself with relatively little left, as long as the bulk of the symbiont has survived. The Alliance learned that lesson the hard way."

Senator Johnston gulped down a huge drink of whiskey

and swallowed. "Why don't we get to the punchline? I want you to spell out clearly what your plan is."

"It's simple. The Vax is powerful, but if we bombard the entire area and turn the land into glass, it won't survive. If we do it immediately upon its arrival, it won't be able to escape, hide or somehow elude our attack."

"Now wait one damned minute," Senator Johnston snapped. "We can't be sure the city will be completely evacuated, let alone our troops."

"This is why I'm telling you this now." There was an edge to Corey's voice. "Pull out your troops. We can't wait for you to evacuate. Any civilians left behind will be unfortunate losses, but this is war."

Senator Johnston slammed his glass on the desk. "I'll admit the evacuation is going better than we hoped, and this is the first time a major city's been evacuated with the aid of such high levels of magic, but that's not the same thing as this city being empty tonight, tomorrow, or even in the next few days. We're talking a lot of people. There are enough gone that our cover-up plans should work, which I would think you would want, given what you've told me about Alliance interactions with the so-called 'more primitive civilizations.' If you kill all those people with an orbital bombardment, I think it'll be kind of hard to explain away."

"This is an unusual situation. It's a matter of galactic security."

Senator Johnston's jaw tightened. "You could at least give us a chance to solve the problem. We have a solution in play."

"Would you prefer we wait until the Vax advances to

another city? They can be fast when they want to. Are you going to evacuate the entire state?"

"The bastard's not that fast. He's practically meandering over on Oriceran."

Corey snorted. "That only means it doesn't have a reason to move quickly yet, or it's trying to gain more adaptations prior to the next part of its mission. If we don't surprise it during its first appearance, we might be forced into a high-mobility situation. I don't think you want the fleet carving up half of California trying to nail the Purifier, and before you say anything, no, we don't trust Brownstone to defeat it. His presence in LA only makes our mission more imperative, but if you want to, tell him to withdraw. We're willing to tolerate that, even if we believe it would be better for your planet and all of ours if he too was destroyed."

Senator Johnston laughed. "You're *willing* to tolerate that? Let me be very clear about what we're discussing. Four Alliance military vessels plan to bombard an American city from orbit without the explicit permission of the United States? Is that what you're telling me, Shepherd? Because it sounds damned outrageous when I say it aloud."

"We're not doing this because we want to. You don't understand. This is a unique opportunity. We have a general idea where and roughly when a powerful Vax might emerge on a target planet. Generally by the time we're forced into this sort of position, the Vax have already laid waste to a significant area. If we wait, it will move on to another city, and it'll happen quicker than you can evacuate it. This is about simple numbers, Senator. Do you want to lose thousands of people, or do you want to lose millions of people? You were elected to help your people, so help them!"

Senator Johnston took slow, measured breaths despite his pounding heart. "Firing weapons of mass destruction against Los Angeles without our explicit permissions means you'll be all but declaring war against the United States. I encourage you to study Article 5 of the NATO Treaty. Declaring war against the United States means declaring war against NATO, and for that matter, I'm pretty sure the Indians, Russians, and Chinese aren't going to be okay with some alien military bombarding our planet from on high, or most countries really. You ready to declare war against the strongest countries on Earth, my alien friend? Because that's what you're talking about doing."

"You'll thank us when it's over," Corey replied. "Even if you don't, it doesn't matter, because we'll have saved you."

"Oh, you believe that crap?" Senator Johnston asked. "You need to spend a lot more time on Earth because you obviously don't understand humans."

"Think about this: you're in a panic because of a single Vax, one that can potentially call others. If you were smart, you'd evacuate everyone but Brownstone and let us to destroy them both."

Senator Johnston scoffed. "You can't honestly believe we would agree to that."

Corey sighed. "You should consider that there's a good possibility the only reason the other Vax is coming is that Brownstone is on Earth. If he's gone, and the Vax are destroyed, there's a good chance they'll never return."

"And if you're wrong, we'll have lost our best weapon

against them other than dropping piles of nuclear weapons on ourselves or letting *helpful* aliens obliterate major metropolitan areas." Senator Johnston stood and shook his head. "You do what you feel is right, *Shepherd*. And we'll do what *we* feel is right. Don't cry when we respond in kind."

"I've given you our warning. That's all I can do. Every human you leave in that area who dies is your responsibility now."

"Interesting perspective. We'll have to agree to disagree. Now, goodnight. I have a few things to take care of." Senator Johnston ended the call and stuck his phone in the pocket of his suit jacket.

You arrogant sons of bitches underestimated Brownstone. Now you're underestimating the United States, and you're going to be sorry about that.

Senator Johnston threw open his door and marched down the hall to the base commander's office. The light was still on, so he knocked.

"Come in," the general ordered.

Senator Johnston pushed open the door and stepped into the room, plastering his best politician smile on his face. "It turns out, General, that we'll have to implement Operation Gulliver, after all."

CHAPTER SEVENTEEN

I've got a few loose ends I should tie up, James thought. *Just in case. Plus, I've got to show my respect. It never hurts to have someone above looking out for you.*

James eyed the coat in the closet. He'd awoken and taken a shower before Shay stirred. For all his bitching about the bed, it ended up being surprisingly comfortable once he bothered to go to sleep.

"I'm gonna go do something," James explained. "You stay here. It shouldn't take long unless the military decides to be stupid."

Shay yawned and sat up, rubbing the sleep out of her eyes. "Are you going to go cause trouble? You should probably save that shit for the Vax. I know we've got a few days still, but half the city's already empty. I doubt you can find a decent warm-up."

James grinned. "Trouble? Nah, far from it. I'm going to church."

"To church?" Shay's confused expression suggested she

couldn't tell if he was joking or serious. "You're going to go to church right now?"

"Yeah. I missed last Sunday, and like you said, we've got some time." James considered for a moment, then grabbed only his holster and gun. An entire tactical vest and accompanying gear might be overkill for the minor pieces of shit he might run into on the streets. He was half-surprised the government had let him keep it all in his room. "I didn't think it was a big deal, but now with all shit happening, it feels like it will be, so I want to go to church."

"I can understand that," Shay replied, her tone placating. "Or at least I can understand why you would believe that, but it's probably already been evacuated. Is it really that important to go an empty building?"

James shrugged. "It is to me. I want my head screwed on right before I cut off the Purifier's."

Shay laughed. "Who knows, it might be the end of the world. Church makes sense. You sure they'll let you leave? Johnston was acting like he didn't want you wandering away too far. He might have made you think you had a choice, but he was implying that you didn't, and he might not think an early-morning prayer session is a good enough reason for you to leave the base."

James finished putting on his holster. "Fuck that. The Vax might come an hour from now, or he might not come for a week, and I've got some thinking to do. The last thing anyone on this base wants right now is to piss me off."

"Okay. You do whatever you need to. Try not to get in any fights with demons on the way." Shay snickered. "Or if you do, make sure they're over quickly. We still need you for the main bout."

"No promises. You know me. I don't go looking for shit, but if it comes to me, I take care of it."

"That you do, James. That you do." Shay laid back down. "Okay, I'm going back to sleep. I'm still worn out from last night, and if the Apocalypse hasn't already started, it's too damned early to get up for less than five million dollars." She offered him a playful grin. "If I'm going to get blown up, sleeping after our fun last night would be a nice way to go out."

James headed down the sidewalk toward the base's front gate, his hands in his pockets. Two Air Force Security Forces personnel manned the small guard post next to the gate, bored looks on their faces as they glumly stared out the window. Given everything going on, he was impressed with their blasé attitude.

Huh. Is it really so different from me most of the time? We have to deal with the shit in front of us. Everyone can get used to anything, given enough time.

James glanced over his shoulder. Much of the base was deserted, with most of the remaining personnel inside helping with whatever schemes and plans Senator Johnston and his government friends had concocted. A single truck turning onto the street in the far distance was one of the few signs of life James had spotted after leaving the mostly-empty barracks.

All non-essential personnel and families had already been evacuated, but a half-dozen drones flew low and circled the base. At least one of the little flying spies had been following him the last couple of minutes.

James didn't give a shit. He wasn't sneaking out, he was leaving in broad daylight. The government wanted his help, and he was happy to give it, but that didn't mean he would ask for permission for everything he did. They didn't own him.

One of the SFs frowned and looked at James as he approached, but the airman kept his rifle slung over his shoulder. "We're on lockdown, sir. Our orders are to not let anyone off the base without explicit permission from above."

"You know who I am, right?" James asked. No matter how many times he assumed his reputation preceded him, sometimes that wasn't the case.

The SFs exchanged glances.

"Mr. Brownstone, we know who you are," the first SF agreed. "We have respect for you and your work, but we've got our orders. Please don't make a scene, sir."

James shook his head, keeping the frustration he felt out of his voice. "And I have somewhere I need to be. You don't want to try to keep me here. We're supposed to be on the same team and shit, but it'll end badly if I have to force my way out. Fuck, you should probably call someone and tell them to give me a ride. It'll be easier to get back then." He turned and waved at the drone following him before gesturing toward the gate.

Just give them different orders, assholes.

The SF opened his mouth, then closed it. He raised his hand to his ear receiver. His brow wrinkled, and he looked at the other guard. They nodded to one another.

"Problem?" James asked. He wasn't in a hurry, but he

didn't want to stand around all day waiting for the Air Force to get their fucking act together. He would like to visit his church before some Vax asshole blew it up.

"Our orders have changed." The SF cleared his throat. "I've been ordered to escort you to the motor pool, Mr. Brownstone."

"Let's get going, then."

James closed the door of the small Air Force truck and stepped outside. The airman inside remained at the wheel, casting confused glances at the Catholic church in the distance. James had given him directions, but he hadn't explained exactly where he was going.

Yeah, I decided I needed to go to church in the middle of the day. Deal with it.

James made his way down the stone path leading to the church. The doors stood open, and he narrowed his eyes. It would be naïve to expect that no one would loot during a mass evacuation, but there were certain desecrations he wouldn't tolerate. He would need to get any looters outside first, so he didn't contribute to the disrespect of the Ultimate Big Man.

The fire left James as he stepped through the entrance hall into the sanctuary. Near the front, Father McCartney knelt in front of the cross, his hands clasped in prayer.

"I didn't expect anyone to be here," James announced. "Especially you. I just thought I should come to pay my respects."

Father McCartney didn't react for several seconds. He

finally stood and crossed himself before turning around. "The National Guard will be coming to pick me up in a few hours. I gave them a rather impassioned speech about spending a few more hours in the church I've served most of my life before its possible destruction."

James nodded. "And the kids?"

"They have all been evacuated to Sacramento, along with the orphanage staff and a few volunteers from the parish who are helping to look after them. Fortunately, your generous donations have allowed me to build up an emergency fund, which is helpful in this...emergency." The priest smiled, looking at the altar. "It's good to know that in dark times, people haven't forsaken the lessons of our Lord. Even if I have no church to come back to, I'll reflect on this experience, knowing that when they were tested, the men and women of the parish did the right thing."

James took a deep breath and slowly let it out. The government might have their secrets and their laws, but God's laws were greater.

"You'll be able to come back to this place," James rumbled. "I'm gonna make sure of that. That's why I'm still around."

Father McCartney nodded slightly, his gaze locked on the other man. He didn't say anything for a long, quiet moment before finally asking, "It's not a lost artifact, is it?"

James shook his head. "It's my fault. My people. They're evil, Father. They live to kill and destroy. Even if I run, they'll follow, and they'll kill everyone in their way, so I have to stand and fight. It's the only way. I have to end this sh..." He sucked in a breath. He needed to remember where he was. "I have to end this."

"No one is completely evil. They've just been denied the light of the Lord and fallen into darkness."

James couldn't help but laugh. "I don't think this is a situation where a few brave missionaries would help, Father. I wish we could talk to them, but the only language they know is violence. The alien who is coming has already killed a lot of people on Oriceran."

Father McCartney offered James a wan smile. "The Church doesn't call for pacifism. It calls for Just War. Remember that even Saint Michael the Archangel had to fight when he and the loyal angels defeated Lucifer and those who would turn against the Lord."

His expression turned grave. "You're right. Sometimes force is the only language evil understands. I will pray for you, James. I will pray for us all, but I also know you, and I know if wicked men, alien or otherwise, would harm the innocent, you will stand against them, and you will show them the power of a man who has kept his faith. If any mortal can save this city, you can." He smiled and knelt in front of the altar. "Now let us pray."

CHAPTER EIGHTEEN

T rey continued down the highway in his F-350, sparing an occasional glance at Zoe. He had been counting on no one trying to stop anyone from entering the city. Several abandoned cars lay on the opposite side of the median, and it had been hours since he had shared the road toward LA with another vehicle. The traffic in the opposite direction remained heavy, but it was moving at a decent rate. He'd seen a lot worse in his life.

Must be a lot of people taking planes or portals out of town. Don't know if that's smarter or dumber, but at least they ain't dumbasses enough to drive back toward town. Like me.

"Shit," Trey muttered.

A military roadblock complete with an armored eight-wheel Stryker vehicle with a heavy machine gun barred his passage. A half-dozen soldiers with rifles at the ready stood behind stripped barricades covered in reflectors.

When they say martial law and mandatory evacuation, they mean it.

Zoe raised a concerned eyebrow.

Trey looked at Zoe. "I've got this. Don't worry."

Zoe smiled. "You're sure you don't want me to cast another tracking spell in case she's moved?"

Trey shook his head. "Nah. Once you did that first one and let me know she was in the general area of her neighborhood, I knew she was at her house. We just got to get there is all, and that'll require more chatting than ass-kicking."

Trey rolled down his window and a soldier approached the car, rifle in hand. "Good morning." He offered the man a charming smile and flipped the mental switch to Smooth Trey.

"Sir, I'm going to have to ask you to turn around," the soldier explained. He nodded up the road. "Just drive over the median and head back. The mandatory evacuation order remains in place."

"You see, here's the problem," Trey responded. "My grandmother is still in town. She got missed during one of the sweeps, and I need to pull her out because she's not gonna leave without a relative grabbing her. She's a stubborn old goat."

"I'm sure your grandmother is fine, sir." The soldier pointed up the road. "So please turn around." A few of the other soldiers frowned.

"Let me lay it out for you, brother." Trey pointed with his thumb at Zoe. "This fine woman right here? She's a witch."

Zoe offered them a wave and a soft smile.

"Um, okay, sir." The soldier frowned, his gaze flicking to the heavy gun of the armored vehicle. "That doesn't change anything. You still need to turn around."

Damn. He thinks Zoe's gonna turn him into a frog or some shit. I could use that, but I don't think that's the way to go. Nah, this guy doesn't look comfortable, especially when I mentioned my grandmother.

"You're not understanding me," Trey explained. "She's a witch, and she's tracked my grandmother to a specific place in the city with magic. I need to get in there and pick my nana up." He gave the soldier a wide grin. "By the way, I'm Trey Garfield with the Brownstone Agency. I can handle myself in there if I run into any trouble."

The soldier looked hesitant. "Sir, this isn't about protecting you from a few stray criminals. It's about the artifact. Trust me, I don't even want to be here right now. They're saying it could do anything from blow up a building to blow up the entire city."

Trey nodded. "I feel you, brother. But that's the thing, you see what I'm saying? If I turn around and leave, knowing, thanks to magic, that my nana is in that city, and she ends up dead because of some big magical bomb? Well, now, I wouldn't get a good night's sleep for the rest of my life. So why don't you let me through? I'm not planning to stay. I'm going right to where she is and grabbing her, and then we're getting the hell out of here. No death wish here for my girlfriend and me. I promise."

The soldier sighed. "Wait here a moment." He turned and jogged over to the front passenger side of the Stryker. The door opened, and he began talking and gesticulating to the officer inside.

Come on. You know you want to let me do this. I don't want to have to run a military blockade to save my nana.

Zoe rested her hands in her lap. "I'll support whatever

you intend to do, but what is your plan should they refuse?"

"We'll drive up a few miles and then drive off the side of the highway or something. Good thing this bad boy has four-wheel drive." Trey patted the dashboard. "We'll get there somehow."

The soldier nodded to the officer and turned around. He waved and yelled something to a few other soldiers, but Trey couldn't make it out.

Trey frowned. "Ain't sure if a quick conversation is a good thing or bad thing, but they don't look like they're gonna ventilate us."

"Always a good thing."

"Shit, yeah."

The soldier didn't return to Trey's truck. He and the other men grabbed the barricades and moved them out of the way. The armored vehicle pulled forward to provide more space.

Trey waited for the soldiers to clear out and gesture him through their new opening. He slowly accelerated and waved.

"Thanks, y'all. I appreciate it."

Trey hopped out of his truck in front of his grandmother's house. Charlyce had been right. Numbers had been painted in white on the front window to indicate the people expected: one, the number found alive: zero, and the number found dead: zero.

Zoe stepped out the opposite side, a cool wind

ruffling her maroon dress. Her breath caught as she surveyed the empty area. "You can almost feel the desperation."

A few discarded wrappers blew up the sidewalk past Trey, and a beer can rolled up the street.

It's like a ghost town already.

Gunfire cracked in the distance, a reminder that the city wasn't empty. Helicopters and military planes flew overhead. Down the street, a covered military truck rumbled past.

Trey and Zoe had passed a few military trucks and armored vehicles on the way to his grandmother's house, but the military vehicles only slowed and let them past without any trouble. He wasn't sure if they checked his license plates and realized he was a Brownstone Agency Bounty hunter or if the officer from the roadblock had passed his request on.

Trey didn't care about the exact reason. He wasn't going to question his good fortune.

Huh. Ain't seen any cops, though. I wonder if they're mostly gone now too?

Trey marched up to the front door and knocked loudly. There was no response.

He threw open the door and stomped inside. "Yo, Nana, you in here? I ain't playing right now. I'm risking getting me and my girlfriend's ass nuked for this."

Zoe sauntered into the house, a slightly amused look on her face. Trey was glad someone was having a good time.

At least we know Nana's alive, thanks to Zoe.

"Nana!" Trey bellowed. "If you don't hurry up, I'm gonna have to start tearing this place up to find you."

"Hush now, boy," Nana Garfield shouted back, her voice muffled. "Don't you dare."

Trey furrowed his brow and looked around. "Where you at?"

A closet door opened and the old woman crept out, cane in one hand, phone in another.

"Why you in there?" Trey asked, frowning.

"Because I heard someone coming, and I thought it might be the soldiers to come to take me away from here again." Nana Garfield sighed before smiling at Zoe. "Hello, dear."

"Hello," Zoe responded softly.

Trey pointed to the open door. "Let's go. You're lucky you ain't already been blown up, hiding in here and lying to Auntie Charlyce. You should be ashamed of yourself. How is that being a good Christian?"

Zoe headed to the porch, content to leave them to solve their family matter without outside interference.

Nana Garfield brandished her cane. "I told you already, boy. I want to die in this house. If I run, what do I have waiting for me? All my memories will go up with this place."

Trey scoffed. "What do you have waiting for you? Are you shitting me now?"

"Watch your mouth, boy." Nana Garfield glared at him.

Trey shook his head and pointed at himself. "This is just a place. Just things. I'm still here. Charlyce is still here, and according to your doctor, you're gonna still be here for a few years yet, and you're getting all up in your head and ready to die because of a house? That's crazy." He scoffed and threw up his hand. "And you know it's crazy. I drove my ass all the way here from Vegas and risked getting shot by some soldiers to come pick you up."

Nana Garfield's expression hardened. "I'm staying."

"We can do this one of two ways," Trey explained. "It's just like when I grab a bounty. We can do it the easy way, and you come along all nice and quiet, or we can do this the hard way, and I drag you kicking and screaming, because I'm not gonna risk leaving you to die. Too many people in my life have gone away, and I refuse to let another one do it because she's stubborn."

His grandmother sighed and looked down. She had teared up. "But what if my house does get blown up?"

"As long as the family that loves you is around, all the houses in the world mean nothing." Trey extended his hand. "Now, come on, Nana. We need to get out of LA before it's too late."

Zoe delicately cleared her throat and stepped inside. "Trey, I would suggest she stay for a few minutes."

"You women are gonna be the death of me." Trey groaned and turned around. "Why?"

"Because there are some rather hard-looking men who just pulled up one house down, and they are now eyeing your truck. They were eyeing me."

Trey scoffed. "What's the damned point of having martial law if you can't even keep a few looters under control?" He reached into his jacket pocket and pulled on his enchanted gloves. "I'll be right back, Nana. You don't need to see this."

The old woman replied with a shallow nod, fear in her eyes. "You be careful, Trey."

Trey headed toward the porch and grabbed the door

handle. "The guys I take down for my job are way tougher than some punk looters. I'll be fine." He slammed the door behind him, more annoyed with the looters for messing up his rescue of his grandmother than anything else.

Zoe was right. Six tattooed toughs piled out of a pickup one house down. Trey was pretty sure at least one of them was an ex-Demon General.

Never get a skull tattoo when you join a gang. It makes it hard if you leave, Mr. Skull Tattoo.

A few had guns tucked in their waistbands.

"Do you need gentlemen need assistance?" Trey called.

The six men sneered and spread out in a rough line. They swaggered toward Trey like they owned the neighborhood.

Look at you motherfuckers. You're the kings of an empty kingdom that might get blown up. You stupid motherfuckers should be mugging refugees in Sacramento or some shit.

"Get the fuck out of here," Mr. Skull Tattoo replied, scratching his butt. "This is our neighborhood, dickwad."

"Nah," Trey replied. "I used to live around here, and this is my nana's house. I ain't recognize any of you motherfuckers, so I figure it's more my neighborhood than yours."

Mr. Skull Tattoo laughed. "You're not getting it, dipshit. We ain't saying we live here. We're saying we're using it for our little shopping trip. Brownstone and his bitches have kept this neighborhood locked up, so you know what I think? I think there's all sorts of shit lying around, because people here have gotten used to the Granite Ghost protecting them. But he ain't here now, is he?"

Trey shook his head. "I think looting when the military's

running around shooting looters and a big bomb might go off is pretty damned stupid. That's what I think." He pointed to a drone in the sky. "Military's probably already coming."

Mr. Skull Tattoo's smile faltered for a moment. "Fuck the military. We ain't had them stop us yet."

"And were you right under a drone before?"

"Fuck you." Mr. Skull Tattoo flipped Trey off. "You ain't nothing, bitch. Get the fuck out of here before we decide to fuck you up."

Trey scratched his cheek. "So, here's how it's gonna go, motherfuckers." He pointed at the house. "This is my nana's house, and if it don't get blown up by some magic bomb, she needs to come back to it, so you need to sit your ugly asses in your truck and get the hell out of here, or you're gonna have to deal with me."

Mr. Skull Tattoo squared his shoulders. "And who the fuck are you? You think you're big shit because you've got some fancy suit on? I'll fuck you up, accountant boy."

I wonder if the big man gets pissed when people don't recognize him? It's fucking annoying.

"'Accountant boy?' What motherfucking accountant wears sweet-ass threads like this? I'm Trey Garfield of the Brownstone Agency, motherfucker." Trey raised his fists. "And you bitches are so pathetic that if you were bounties, I wouldn't even bother with you myself. I'd send one of our new guys to pick you up. Maybe we should get some interns from the local high school for pieces of trash like you."

Mr. Skull Tattoo nodded to his friends and slammed his fist into his palm. "Don't kill him, boys. I want him to lie there, all battered and busted up, as we rip that old piece-of-shit house apart."

"Some fuckers learn easily," Trey intoned. "Others need the lesson smashed into their motherfucking skulls." He sprinted forward and brought back his fist.

The looters swarmed him in a half-circle. Trey threw a punch into the face of a thug on his right, and the blow sent the man flying backward. His friends gawked in surprise, or perhaps fear, after the sickening crunch accompanying the attack.

Trey didn't pause to gloat. His elbow strike cracked the ribs of another man. Two quick jabs disoriented another two thugs and sent them stumbling back. A final jump-kick ended with another man hitting the ground and smashing his head into the sidewalk.

The lone unwounded looter, Mr. Skull Tattoo, went for his gun. Trey grabbed his arm and bent it back until it snapped. The man howled in pain.

Trey yanked the thug's head down and brought up his knee, and blood blurted from the thug's face as his nose broke. Two brutal follow-up blows robbed the man of his consciousness. Trey let the trash fall to the ground where he belonged.

The remaining conscious looters moaned in pain, backing away from Trey.

"If you didn't win with all your guys, you ain't gonna win with fewer," Trey observed. "That's just fucking math, bitch."

The men not grimacing in pain glared at Trey.

"I'm not gonna waste your asses," he explained, "because I don't want my nana walking outside her house and finding bodies. She's having a hard time right now, and she don't need that shit." He kicked Mr. Skull Tattoo, and his body rolled over. "So unless you assholes want me to beat you all down, you take your wounded, you get in your truck and you never, ever come back here. You dumb motherfuckers should get the fuck out of the city before you get your asses nuked."

The grimacing thugs picked up their wounded and backed slowly toward their truck, their gazes locked on Trey.

Trey watched them go, his hands twitching and ready to go for his gun if they decided to be stupid. They loaded into their truck, piling their unconscious men in the back seat. The truck roared to life and sped down the street.

A military drone skimming the nearby roofs zoomed after the truck.

Trey sighed, then hurried back to the porch and opened the front door. "Let's get the hell out of here."

"What if they come back?" Nana Garfield asked.

"They ain't coming back. They lucky if the National Guard don't gun their asses down." Trey offered his hand. "But I wanted to make it clear that no one messes with my nana's house."

Two hours later, Zoe and the Garfields were halfway to Vegas on I-15N. Nana Garfield slept in the backseat, snoring loudly.

Zoe had been smirking at Trey for the last ten minutes.

"What?" Trey finally asked. "Why you looking at me like that? It's making me nervous."

"Oh, my little supernova, you continue to impress. You drove back into great danger for a relative who was ready to die."

Trey scoffed. "I ain't leaving my nana to get vaporized and shit, that's for fucking sure. And what about you? You came with me. Who's dumber? The person who does dumb shit, or the person who follows them?"

Zoe laughed, the sound almost musical. "A good question. I think I've spent too many years forgetting what it means to truly live. With you, I feel alive again, and it's not just your energy. It'll be fun having your relatives stay with us." She smiled at Nana Garfield. "My world's more interesting with you around, Trey."

Trey grinned. "Glad to hear that."

Okay, I've taken care of what's mine. Now it's up to you, big man. I don't know what you can do, but if you can do anything, save Nana's house.

Shit, might as well save the rest of LA while you're at it.

CHAPTER NINETEEN

James had never thought he would so look forward to a meeting, but after a day of sitting around in the barracks room, doing anything, even going to another room, sounded like a good idea, even with Shay distracting him.

An armed airman escorted James through the maze-like hallways of one of the base buildings.

I just want this shit over, and we still have several more days before that fucker shows up. I can't even concentrate on barbeque. Fuck. That's just messed up.

Fucking Vax. Invade my planet and distract me from barbeque?

The airman escorting James gestured to an open door as they arrived at their location.

Senator Johnston sat inside, along with several military officers and various other people in suits James didn't recognize or care about. They were in the middle of an animated discussion when he entered. Everyone stopped talking and looked at him.

James grunted and sat in an empty corner seat.

"Thank you for joining us, Mr. Brownstone," Senator Johnston offered. "I'll cut through the bullshit. Our boy on Oriceran is no longer doing his tourist imitation. He's now started jumping, taking these big leaps like we've seen you do. It's not the most graceful thing in the world, but he's definitely sped up. Way up."

James frowned. "How soon until he hits that resonance place?"

"By our current estimates, twelve hours."

"Do you have any idea where he might come out?" James' hands curled into fists under the table. Twelve hours until he met one of his people. Twelve hours until he found out if he had a destiny, or if he would just be another victim of the Vax.

Senator Johnston nodded. "Sometimes luck smirks a little even as she's kicking you in the balls. The Oricerans have pinpointed what they believe is a possible exit point. It's likely going to be near USC."

James frowned. "Near USC? I don't think I came to Earth originally near USC unless shit was way different thirty years ago."

"I don't know what to tell you, son. I'm just telling you what the magical folks have told me. They passed along a bunch of mumbo-jumbo, but it all amounts to that's their best guess."

"We should get me over there then."

"Not yet," General Hallwell, the base commander, interjected. "That's not a good plan."

James furrowed his brow. "If we know where he's

gonna come out, why not let me be there to welcome his ass to Earth Brownstone-style?"

"This Oriceran intelligence comes with caveats," the general replied. "We've discussed this with Senator Johnston, and we don't think it's a good idea. You have to understand, Mr. Brownstone, the evacuation, as well as it's gone, is still far from complete. Thousands of civilians remain in LA. The Army is making sure the area near USC is clear, but we need you to remain on standby until such time as the bastard comes through and we know his exact position. Everything we know about Vax military capabilities suggests he'll be able to initiate an immediate offensive. We don't want to waste precious minutes."

Senator Johnston nodded. "I concur."

James' gaze swept the table and passed over all the concerned government officials and military officers. "I've got a better suggestion if this is about getting me to him for quicker ass-kicking."

"We're listening."

"Put me up in a chopper here about an hour before the bastard hits the resonance zone. If I'm already in the air, the chopper can take me wherever he shows up. I'll be ready." James growled. "And I'll make this fucker regret ever setting foot on Earth."

General Hallwell nodded and turned to a major sitting beside him. "Get that going."

The other officer stood and rushed out of the room.

Senator Johnston also stood. "I suppose I need to get ready for my part in this."

"Which is what?" James asked.

"Keeping the Nine Systems Alliance honest," Senator

Johnston explained. "Let's just say I give you my personal guarantee that the only thing you'll need to deal with, son, is your disagreeable relative."

James grunted. "Good. I don't want to have to watch my fucking back. You sure you can do that, though?"

"Of course. We hired the best people to get us what we needed to be ready for the Alliance, just like we've hired the best people to help us fight the Vax." Senator Johnston opened the door. "I'm hoping that by tonight you can go back to worrying about your wedding plans, Mr. Brownstone. I got the Save-the-Date, by the way. I do appreciate it."

"No problem," James rumbled. "Don't worry. Our venue's not gonna be in LA. Even if this place gets blown up, we're good."

Senator Johnston laughed. "Well, now, that's one positive way to spin the situation."

Fleet Commander Laralan stared at the holographic image of Earth floating in front of him as he sat in his command chair on the bridge. He wouldn't deny the beauty of the blue planet. It was cruel fortune that had forced him to lead this fleet to the system on a mission of destruction.

Maybe the Spirits chose me to make up for the last Shepherd's mistake.

Other than being the same species as the last Shepherd, the commander had no relationship to her. He hadn't even suffered like she had, having lived far away from any world ravaged by the Vax.

Still, the commander kept returning to the same conclusion. If Aiyn or her successor had done their jobs, Brownstone would no longer be on Earth, and Laralan wouldn't be forced into having to order its bombardment.

Clicks and buzzes sounded from his insectoid Techain helmsman, the sounds hollow inside his breather helmet. "In position, Commander," came the translation. His clawed, jointed fingers made several quick motions in the air, manipulating virtual controls only he could see thanks to projections inside his helmet.

"Show me," Laralan ordered.

The holographic image of the Earth was replaced by an overlay graphic indicating the fleet was near the planet's moon. They were preparing for a hard burn that would allow them to establish a proper geostationary orbit over the target city. From there, it was a simple matter of initiating the bombardment.

Laralan narrowed his eyes. Shepherd 8224's last report indicated that thousands of civilians remained in the city.

May the Spirits forgive me for what I'm about to do.

CHAPTER TWENTY

James tossed his coat and holster on the desk in the barracks room. There was no reason to bring a gun to fight the Purifier.

Shay sat on the edge of the bed with a frown on her face. "I still wish I could help you."

"Some fights a man has to undertake by himself," James replied. "They're going to come here in a few minutes to get me to the helicopter. I'm sure if I asked Johnston, he could airlift you out of Los Angeles."

Shay snorted. "No fucking way." She smirked. "You just want an excuse, don't you?"

"Huh? An excuse? What are you talking about?"

Shay hopped off the bed and pointed at him. "An excuse to lose."

James grunted. "I'm not looking for an excuse to lose. I just thought it'd be safer for you."

"No. I'm not going anywhere. I don't want, even for a second, some part of your mind to think you have an out. If I'm gone, you might think, 'Hey, I can always fall back.'"

Shay shook her finger. "That goes for the wish, too. That's Alison's. Don't be a pussy and steal it just because the Purifier gets in a few good hits."

"If I have to use the wish to survive, the fight would just end with him kicking my ass a second time anyway." James shrugged. "I'll take him out without it."

In truth, the only time he'd even thought of the wish lately was when he was talking to Shay about fighting the Drow. She was right. Any fight he approached thinking he might have a backup or a reset for was a fight he was already losing mentally. That might not be a problem normally because he outclassed almost everyone he ran into, but going up against another Vax, he would need to go into battle thinking there were only two choices: victory or death.

Shay walked up to him and put her hands on his cheeks. "You just win, damn it. You pound this fucker into tiny little pieces until no one can even figure out what he originally was, and then you come back to me. Because I love you, and I didn't love anyone before I met you. Shit, I didn't even love myself. Don't make me fucking regret that, and don't think I can't figure out a way to chase you into the afterlife to harass you for fucking this up."

James grinned. "Yeah, I'll keep that in mind."

Shay pressed her mouth to his for a deep kiss, and its heat blew out the few other worries James had. He reluctantly pulled away.

"I love you too, Shay," James replied, the low bass of his voice almost a growl.

Someone knocked on the door. "Mr. Brownstone, the helicopter's ready for you."

Shay reached into her pocket and pulled out three small rings. She offered them to him in his palm. "All magic. Mostly glorified night lights, but I always carry a few on me in case you need a little boost. You know what you need to do."

James scooped up the rings and put them in his pocket.

It was time. He reached under his shirt and removed the spacer.

The pain of the bonding was like a distant dream as James' thoughts focused on everything he had to defend: his church, his city, his woman, his daughter, his planet. He had been born a Vax, but he had lived his life as a human, and it was time to prove his loyalty.

Not only that, it was time to prove who was the toughest son of a bitch on the planet.

Initiation, Whispy sent.

It's time to achieve the primary directive. It's time to waste another Vax symbiont.

Yessss, Whispy hissed in satisfaction.

"That's all well and good, Angus," the President explained over the phone, "and winning against both sets of aliens sounds at least possible, but we still have to consider the aftermath and how it might change things. It does us no good to solve this situation, only to have planetary riots the next day."

"Yes, sir," Senator Johnston replied as he marched down the hallway. An open portal stood at the end, four wizards from the PDA standing to either side. "I'm well aware of that, but I can assure you we not only have our top magical personnel on the issue, but the Oricerans have been very generous in terms of providing additional magical resources for all the illusion magic we need."

The President sighed. "I still don't understand. Won't people know because of what has happened on Oriceran? Your reports have been unclear on that."

"That's the funny thing. They're not so keen to advertise what's going on either, and Ambassador Yona assures me they'll take care of everything on their end. The truth is, strange, powerful beings aren't as much an oddity there." Senator Johnston adjusted his phone slightly for comfort. "So, yes, the attack will be discussed, but as long as we win here, they can write it off on their end with a cover story about sending the enemy to the World in Between. It's not like they have websites blasting news 24/7 over there. In some ways, it's easier to manage the spread of information there despite all the magic."

The President sighed. "And what about satellites?"

"Right now, one of the most impressive illusions in probably hundreds of years is covering greater LA area. It's not like we can hide that magical signature, but the Broken Wand excuse gives people a reason to understand why they might sense it. We've also initiated warding and other techniques to keep the truth to people on a need-to-know basis." Senator Johnston slowed to a stop in front of the portal. "If all goes well, no one who doesn't need to know will ever find out what happened. Yes, there will be conspiracy theories for years, but they'll never figure it out. Who could even believe the truth? Different aliens, Brownstone being an alien? Hell, *I* barely believe it, and I know it's true."

"And if it goes wrong?"

Senator Johnston laughed. "Well, that's what I'm for, now, isn't it? Don't worry, sir, we've got this handled. I've got to get going. It's time for me to go meet our other new friends."

An opaque dark portal ripped open over a sidewalk near the corner of Jefferson and Vermont. Any other day, hundreds of witnesses have would been present to gawk at the unusual sight. That day, only a few stray dogs across the street jerked their heads up from their bountiful feast to check out the strange phenomenon. The evacuation had left local garbage cans laden with delicious treats for the hungry animals.

The metallic silver-green armored leg of the Purifier emerged through the portal, followed by the rest of his body. The dogs whimpered and fled, sensing the murderous intent of the new arrival. The portal closed behind the Vax.

A few drones circled overhead, relaying their information to the military. They lasted for a few more seconds before the Vax blasted out energy bolts that ripped through them, reducing them to falling chunks of melted metal and plastic.

The Purifier's loud roar sent the birds in nearby trees into the sky in a huge mass. The Vax didn't bother firing at them. Instead, he turned toward a cement and brick apartment complex nestled in some trees nearby.

The deadly alien channeled energy through both his arm blades and appendages. He released the built-up energy as one massive blast that screamed through the trees and struck the side of the apartment building. The massive explosion blew half the building apart, the shockwave knocking down several nearby trees.

The Vax invasion of Earth had begun.

CHAPTER TWENTY-ONE

Commander Laralan strained against his seat straps. It was a bad habit from his younger days whenever a battle was approaching. An orbital bombardment might not constitute a true battle, but it was close enough for his heart and brain.

The command center was a large triangular room with a half-dozen stations nestled in the heart of the ship. Most of the dark chairs didn't look impressive, other than a few adaptive displays and controls on the armrests, but they all sent data feeds directly to ocular implants or generated active displays directly in front of the crew member manning the station. Virtual displays made it easy to customize the individual stations for missions.

Commander Laralan didn't see why they needed so much non-functional empty space, but from what he had read, Alliance psychological research had indicated that it was helpful for successful integration of the various different species who might serve on an Alliance ship. Not every species liked to be close to one another, and the ones who did, also didn't mind the opposite.

The commander tried to push the trivia out of his mind. It wasn't long until their deadly mission. He'd participated in orbital bombardments before, but never against a target where so many civilians were still in place.

He was also surprised. Despite all the bluster of the human authorities, there was no indication they would have trouble engaging the target zone. The humans had somehow cloaked the area to hide the presence of the Vax, but from what the Alliance could make out from their probe, there was no actual defensive shields extended over the city. Commander Laralan wasn't sure if humans could achieve something like that, even with magic.

"Massive energy surge above the planet, sir," reported the sensor operator, a blue-skinned member of the commander's own species—another person who would atone for the previous Shepherd's failures.

Commander Laralan frowned. "What's going on?" His restraints kept him in place when he instinctively tried to stand. This wasn't the time for pacing. He tapped his AllBand to bring up a status display.

"I don't know, Commander. These readings are similar in some ways to Vax portals, but the scale of the energy involved is massively different. There are also numerous phase differences."

"Comms, signal the fleet, high alert, maximum defensive posture." Laralan watched the overlay on his display depicting the position of the ships, along with a new symbol representing the energy surge. "I doubt the Vax have suddenly learned a new trick and are going to spit out a ship at us." He tapped on the graphic floating in front of him to obtain a magnified visual. "This means the natives are up to something."

A swirling portal sat above the Earth in the image. Bands of shimmering colors pulsed across the strange hole in reality. "It doesn't look like a Vax portal at all. It also doesn't look like the ones we've been briefed on, even before considering the size." Laralan narrowed his eyes. "All ships, prepare for attack. I don't think this is the Vax. I think the humans are being clever. I'm guessing they'll launch missiles or magical attacks from the surface through this portal. Ready active defenses."

Laralan shook his head, glad the fleet hadn't launched any fighters. He could respect the human forces for trying to defend their planet, even if their plan was feeble, doomed, and desperate. Some of their larger nuclear weapons might stand a chance of breaking through at least some of the ships' defensive fields, but there was no way the fleet would let the primitive projectiles get close. Point-defense beams would tear them to pieces well outside the blast radius. It would be a glorious light show, but nothing more. The scale of magical attacks available to them wouldn't be a problem either.

"The readings are changing, Commander," the sensor operator reported. "I think... Wait. Something's coming through."

"Impress me, humans," the commander muttered. A few seconds later, he magnified the visual again, confused. "What is that?"

Laralan expected a swarm of nuclear missiles to emerge or even a swarm of high-speed railgun rounds. A mass of magical fireballs wouldn't have surprised him. Nothing like that came out of the portal.

A strange new arrival floated out of the portal, an island of stone covered by a glowing translucent orb. Terraced towers with curved, tiled roofs in a myriad of colors lay in concentric circles around a central golden ziggurat. A faceted dome of blue crystal lay at the summit.

"What's the size of that thing?" Laralan barked, still having trouble understanding what he was seeing. His mind strained to find a point of comparison.

The sensor operated rattled off some numbers. The strange object was about half as long as one of his ships, and much wider.

That was exactly what it had to be—a ship, despite its bizarre appearance. This was the true threat of magic, one he had underestimated.

Commander Laralan wouldn't have cared if lightning or fire had come through the portal. Generating understandable attacks using forces known to normal physics through unusual means didn't confound him, but how was he supposed to respond to the temple island in front of his fleet? It wasn't like he'd trained for this. Even the Vax didn't behave in such an absurd manner.

"Does it have anything that might be a weapons system?" Laralan asked.

The sensor operator's hands continue to fly over the virtual controls. "I can't tell, Commander. The outer energy field is disrupting most of the sensor readings, and there are no obvious external launchers. The object is moving at a minimal relative speed. There is no sign of active propulsion."

The stone island floated away from the portal. Once the island cleared it completely, the portal vanished.

Laralan ordered the fleet to hold position. The island might be some sort of magical bomb, but there was no way the humans could hope to take out his entire fleet. The distances were just too vast. That was the problem with primitive species who wanted to play in space; their intuition failed them when they tried to analyze it.

A wavering image winked into existence near the front of the commander center, as if someone were projecting a picture on flowing water. The image depicted a stone wall filled with inscriptions in some language Laralan didn't recognize.

He was about to ask who had brought up the odd display when an elderly human in a suit stepped into frame, an easy and disarming smile on his face. The commander recognized the man from the reports Shepherd 8224 passed along: the American senator, Angus Johnston.

The fleet commander tapped his AllBand to activate real-time translation, still frustrated that the humans had taken him so thoroughly by surprise.

Senator Johnston's smile broadened. "Well, now, this is quite nice." He looked around "They said it'd be like looking right into your ship, and it's just like that, but they might have made a mistake, so before we continue, I need to establish that I'm talking to whoever is in charge of the Alliance Fleet. The magicals tell me the spell is supposed to open up to whoever is most important, but that's such a relative thing. For all I know, this is your religious ship or the man who supplies all the food."

"I am Fleet Commander Laralan, and I'm in command of these four vessels." The commander frowned. "While we talk, a Vax is laying waste to your city. I don't know what sort of trick this is, Senator, but any delay that costs a human life will be your fault."

"That's very much true, and trust me, it's weighing heavily on my mind." Senator Johnston shrugged. "But the Vax is blowing away empty buildings right now. Not sure if we'll be able to fix it, but I've got some ideas about that." He shook a finger. "You don't worry about that ornery fellow. I've got my own ornery fellow who will be handling him soon enough."

"What is this…thing you've deployed?" Commander Laralan asked, venom is his tone. He didn't like the human's flippant attitude. "A bomb?"

"Now that's the other problem with your Alliance. All that fancy technology, but not a drop of magic. I get why you're so scared, but the smart play would have been not to piss us off rather than to threaten us." Senator Johnston gestured toward the inscriptions in the wall. "Your lack of magic means you don't get cool toys like this—one of the most powerful of the ancient vimanas. That's what this thing is called, by the way." He sighed. "I'll tell you one thing: when I was a boy, I never thought I would ever fly around in a magical castle in space chatting with aliens. The world has changed."

"You're on it, then?" Commander Laralan was impressed that the human leader would risk himself, but disappointed by how foolish the man had been by revealing the fact. If the fleet took out the vimana, Earth's anti-Alliance faction would be in disarray.

Senator Johnston nodded. His image wavered so much he was hard to discern for a few seconds, but then it settled back to normal. "Now, I'm not going to spend time lying to you because you've got that little spy on our planet who hears things, so let me be very clear about this, Commander. Right now, I've got the full magical might of the elite magicals who serve the United States, along with more than a few friendly Oricerans fueling this thing. I don't want to have to give you a good, old-fashioned whupping, because I understand that you think you're doing the right thing. But so are we."

"One magical ship won't be able to stop this fleet, but if you fire on us, we will defend ourselves. I've also read the Shepherd's reports, and I'm well aware that magic is weaker once you leave the planet. Your tricks might have been useful if we were intending to land ground forces, but our current mission will continue. I doubt your magical toy even has the necessary offensive capabilities to destroy any of our ships."

Senator Johnston looked impressed. "Sadly, you're correct. For all the fancy magical wards and glyphs and whatnot inside this thing, it doesn't actually have any weapons. I figured it'd at least have a nice lightning beam or something like that."

Commander Laralan frowned. "You're attempting to turn my fleet back with an unarmed vessel? I admire your courage, Senator, even if it's wasted in this pointless endeavor. We don't have time for this farce. If you don't have anything useful to add to our conversation, then we'll continue on our way to save your planet from the monster now ravaging it."

Senator Johnston shook his head. "I'm sorry, but I can't allow that. You see, there are plenty of different ways to stop strong foes. It's a big thing in Earth culture for all sorts of different traditions. In my country, a lot of people grow up hearing about David versus Goliath. You know that story, Commander?"

Commander Laralan shook his head. "I'm a military commander, not a Shepherd or a diplomat. I'm not an expert on Earth culture."

"The more you know about a culture, the more you know about how they might fight back. I won't bother you with the fine details of the story, other than to note that a weaker man defeated a stronger man when the stronger man had every reason to expect he would win."

Commander Laralan looked to his side, where a smooth-headed, spindly, pale, silver-eyed female humanoid sat. She was his comms officer.

This was what the humans didn't understand. The Alliance fleet didn't represent a single planet or race, but nine different species who had come together over the centuries to be stronger and better. The Vax were one of the few true threats to their continued cooperation and advancement. The commander couldn't let human stubbornness allow a major threat to escape, even if he had to earn some enmity.

"Comms, notify the fleet to prepare to enter orbit and prepare for bombardment," Commander Laralan barked. "This human is just stalling for time."

Senator Johnston laughed and clapped. "Yes, my alien friend, I was in fact stalling for time."

Commander Laralan glared at the human. This situation was serious, and Senator Johnston was acting like it was an amusing game to him. The human's own people were about to die, and he was showing no respect. Disgusting.

"You've accomplished nothing," Commander Laralan explained. "Again, I'm sorry for what we have to do. It brings me no pleasure, not that it seems to bother you."

Senator Johnston clucked his tongue. "You won't be getting anywhere near Earth. You're going to stop and fly back to the moon until James Brownstone is done introducing a little liberty and justice for all to that Vax. If you don't, I'm afraid we're going to have to destroy your fleet."

"I don't know much about Earth or American culture, Senator, but it's hard to make threats when you already admitted you don't have weapons. On my planet, you don't make threats you can't back up."

"I never said I didn't have weapons. I just said this vimana doesn't have any offensive weapons. It's useful in a different way." Senator Johnston's annoying grin returned.

"And what's that?"

Senator Johnston glanced to his side and nodded at someone off-screen. "For one thing, it's a nice big collective relay for magical power. The great part about it is you don't even have to have all the magicals on the damned thing to relay their power."

Commander Laralan frowned, unsure if he should order the fleet to destroy the vimana or bypass it. If the vimana could act as a bomb, as he suspected, the humans might be channeling magical power into it for a suicide attack.

"Comms, order the fleet to—"

Two portals appeared in different corners of the bridge. Before Fleet Commander Laralan could get off a command, wizards and witches in dark fatigues rushed out, their wands up, glowing magical forcefields spread out in front of them.

The bridge's security guard pulled out a pulse pistol and aimed at the closest invader. He fired off a blast, a bright crackle of white energy, but it struck the shield and disappeared in a flash. The commander yanked out his own pistol and pointed the weapon at another intruder.

A single American Marine in an exoskeleton emerged from each of the portals with a railgun in hand. A third Marine appeared with no weapon, holding up a large black metal box with the help of the exoskeleton. He set it down. "This is Eagle Four. The Roman Candle has been delivered, Sky Castle."

"Get more security up here!" Commander Laralan ordered. He glared at Senator Johnston. "This was your brilliant plan? Use magic to send a few troops and take the bridge? This mission will continue even if you kill me and the other commanders."

Senator Johnston shook his head. "No, you misunderstand. This isn't about killing you. This is about obliterating your entire fleet. Let me lay it out for you: on each of your four ships, there is now a similar team. The last man who entered is carrying what we call on Earth a suitcase nuke." He scoffed. "Of course, we need a Marine in an exoskeleton to easily carry the thing. Anyway, I'm guessing that all your fancy technology might help you survive a nuke if we fired it from the outside, but it probably won't do much if we set it off on the inside."

"This is a trick," Commander Laralan shouted, still pointing his weapon at a nearby stone-faced witch.

"Do some fancy alien scan if you don't believe me." Senator Johnston snorted. "Also, let me introduce another Earth concept to you: a dead man switch. There's a spell on the devices. If everyone on one of those teams dies, boom. If the vimana gets taken out, boom. We can die together, my alien friend, but no one has to."

The commander lowered his weapon, looked at his sensor operator, and nodded.

The sensor operator swallowed as his hands flew over the virtual controls. He grimaced and returned the nod.

Commander Laralan' eyes bulged. "Do you understand what you're doing, human? Do you have any concept? There are thousands of Alliance personnel on these ships."

Senator Johnston's smile vanished, replaced by a mask of rage. "And you're threatening to kill thousands of Americans, civilian and military," he shouted, his face reddening. "Don't you dare lecture me about killing people unnecessarily when you're sitting above my planet with warships, ready to raze one of our cities."

"No, we're going to protect your planet. Some sacrifices are necessary for the greater good."

Senator Johnston scoffed. "You back the hell up and let Brownstone do his thing, or you're going to have to make the ultimate sacrifice for your mission."

The human and the alien stared at each other, both wearing their anger openly.

"Your people would die too," Commander Laralan noted.

"Yes, they would." Senator Johnston's expression softened. "Which is unfortunate, but they're all volunteers who knew what they signed up for. They're willing to do what they need to protect their country from your particular foreign threat."

The magicals and Marines stood tall, their wands and weapons at the ready. One of the Marines gave a curt nod to Commander Laralan.

Even if the alien didn't understand everything about Earth, he knew the look of a warrior ready to die to defend his homeland. Some things were universal.

"Send an order to the fleet," Commander Laralan began. "We'll pull back to the moon and let the humans sacrifice unnecessary lives while they place their trust in a remorseless killer."

Senator Johnston's fake smile returned. "No, we're placing our faith in a flawed but good man. Don't worry, though. It's not like we don't have a few cards left to play."

CHAPTER TWENTY-TWO

"Sir." The pilot of the helicopter spoke through his headset to James. "We've got eyes on the target. It is currently near Jefferson and Vermont, about five minutes away. Target has demonstrated anti-air capability and taken out all the drones in the area, but they still have it on stationary local cameras."

"Jefferson and Vermont?" James chuckled. He was strapped into a seat in the back of the small utility helicopter. The concrete and steel jungle zoomed past below him. "So the Oricerans were right and the fucker is near USC. I wonder if Shay will be happy if we bust up her rival school."

"Sir?"

"Don't worry about it," James replied. "You can't get too close. He'll take you out, and this thing is a lot larger than a drone."

"We're going to stay low, sir. I'll get you in nice and close. Hold on tight." The helicopter banked and dove, passing between two high-rise buildings.

James growled. "Fuck that. You make sure you're out of the line of fire. Just get me a few minutes closer, and I'll bail from there. I can move pretty fast once I start. The area's clear, right? Because if I need to let loose, I don't want to have to worry about random people wandering in."

"Far as I know, sir."

Engage and kill primary enemy, Whispy demanded.

Yeah, we're gonna do that, but I'm not gonna sacrifice this pilot on the way.

Plumes of smoke rose from all over the city, most having nothing to do with the alien. The Vax might have begun his assault, but the passive damage from millions of people fleeing for their lives had already been done. The helicopter waggled back and forth to avoid buildings and smoke.

Military vehicles roamed the streets, and the occasional squad of soldiers on foot rushed up a road a hundred feet below the helicopter. A smattering of civilian vehicles screamed down the empty streets. Even rarer, some people stepped out of a building to watch the skies.

Too many people still here. Fucking Purifier got too eager. Why couldn't you have waited a week?

Kill the enemy, Whispy responded. *Achieve primary directive.*

Green light flashed in the distance. Something exploded in the air miles ahead, the smoke and debris trails visible.

"Shit," the pilot.

James pulled the rings out of his pocket. "What's going on?"

"Apparently, they were trying a Storm run, sir. The

target blew it out of the sky." The pilot sounded more angry than afraid.

"Storm run?"

"Big-ass close-attack semi-autonomous support platform, sir. The thing's more bomb than plane."

Idiots. All you're doing is helping him adapt more. Leave this shit to me.

James grunted. "Okay, how far out are we now?"

"About two minutes, sir."

The cloud of thick, dark smoke straight ahead marked the position of the Purifier. Another massive green blast erupted in the distance and struck a nearby building, and the top of the building fell to the ground in a shower of metal and glass.

The only thing preventing worse destruction was the modest height of the nearby buildings, but the Purifier was only a couple of miles from the heart of downtown LA and a whole forest of skyscrapers to cut down.

I need to stop this asshole before he really gets moving or just decides to fire in that direction.

"Stop here," James ordered. "You get any closer, you're fucking dead. Put me down here."

"Roger that, sir," the pilot replied.

The helicopter descended until it was hovering twenty feet off the ground.

"Good luck, sir," the pilot offered. "I wish I had taken the time to get your autograph."

James grinned from the back. "Look me up later and I'll give you one." He removed his headset, unbuckled his restraints, and jumped out of the helicopter, landing in a crouch.

The aircraft rose into the sky, its spinning blades kicking up the dust and rocks. The steady thump drowned out all other sounds as it turned around and fled the engagement zone.

It was time to get to work.

James grabbed the rings Shay had given him and pressed them against his amulet.

Drain them, and let's go extended advanced, James ordered.

Alternative power source detected. Power sufficient for extended advanced transformation.

The biometallic tendrils shot from the amulet and coated James' body. His helmet closed around his head, blinding him for a moment before his expanded range of vision came online. Twin blades extended from his arms, along with claws.

James took a few deep breaths. No rage or anger filled him, even as he prepared to face off against the Purifier. He was focused and ready to kick the visitor's ass, but he was banking on his *human* mind to help him win. Whispy's adaptations had given him advantages over the years, but maintaining control of the host-symbiont relationship might prove to be the most important of all of them.

Everything James knew about the Vax suggested the host became nothing more than a meat puppet, needed more for their body and cellular structure than their personality or consciousness. Maybe Whispy was unusual, but if he was at all representative of symbionts, they were good at adaptation but not necessarily any good at tactics. If the enemy was a mindless killer, James could use that against him.

Active symbiont signature detected, Whispy reported. *Purifier transformation detected.*

James snorted as another explosion shot flame and smoke into the sky.

Yeah, not worried about finding him. If you can sense him, he can sense me, and even though he's making a big fucking show, he's here for me. Let's go say hello to the fucker.

James sprinted and leapt, his enhanced armored legs pushing him high into the air. He landed and jumped again; poor man's flight, but he would arrive at the location of the Purifier within minutes, no helicopter needed.

A leap took him over several tanks parked in a line, their main guns pointed in the general direction of the Purifier. After a few more jumps, even the soldiers and military vehicles disappeared, leaving an empty expanse of concrete and glass—a hive of humanity without any people. There was nothing eerier than an empty city.

The heavy clouds of smoke loomed larger as James continued his travel toward the Vax. A green beam shot from the ground and swept through the area, slicing buildings in half. The entire area shook from the collapsing debris, and so much fire and debris now choked the air, it was hard to remember this was the middle of Los Angeles and not some blasted war-torn overseas hellhole.

In a matter of minutes, the Purifier had already broken James' record for property damage, but that was just another grievance to add to the list. Whispy continued his demands for battle, but given that James was heading straight toward the enemy, he wasn't sure if this was the symbiont's version of murderous cheerleading.

James let out a low growl as he hurtled between some

buildings. He hoped approaching the monster would get it to at least stall its attack.

"I'm not on your side, asshole," James muttered. "And I'm about to prove it."

Another leap sent him flying through the air. He cleared a low-lying building and saw the outline of his enemy. The armored form of the Purifier was obscured by thick smoke. Whatever endless light-years separated Earth from the Vax home world, only a hundred yards now remained between Earth's Forerunner and the Vax Purifier.

Time to achieve the primary directive, James thought.

Whispy beamed excitement into his mind.

CHAPTER TWENTY-THREE

James marched down the street toward the Purifier, smoke and burning trees and buildings forming walls on either side. The other Vax walked forward. Neither armored man displayed any sense of urgency, their steps steady but slow, but at least the Purifier ceased his attacks. James' immediate plan had worked.

Engage and destroy the enemy, Whispy demanded.

We're gonna give him one chance to do this the easy way.

Achieve primary directive, Whispy insisted.

Shut it and get ready.

James continued closing on his opponent. The other Vax stood a good foot taller than him. He wasn't sure if that meant the Purifier's armor was bulkier, or if the host was taller. The two twitching shoulder appendages were one obvious point of departure. There was something very disgusting and insect-like about them.

"I should kick your ass for what you've done already," James bellowed, his voice amplified by his helmet, "but I'm gonna give you one chance to leave here alive. Since you came here through a portal, I'm betting you can leave the same way, and not back via Oriceran, but all the way back to wherever the fuck you came from. If not, then we're gonna have painful conversation that's gonna end with you dead and your symbiont crying before I destroy it too."

The Purifier responded with a bestial roar. He spread his arms and curled his clawed hands into fists, and his blades and claws retracted. A high-pitched whine followed.

What the fuck is that? James thought, unsure if the Purifier was pissed or ready to cooperate. He concentrated, and his own blades and claws disappeared. Talking it out wasn't his style, but it wouldn't hurt to try.

Symbiont data adaptation sharing request, Whispy explained. *Direct contact necessary.*

Wait, you telling me that if that fucker touches me, he gets all your adaptations?

No. Agreement necessary for symbiont adaptational sharing without override.

James grunted. The next few seconds would determine if he could defend the Earth after all his big talk. The fate of the planet might come down to the loyalty of a violence-obsessed alien biotechnological symbiont.

So the fucker wants my hard-earned secrets, James thought. *But I think he's a lazy son of a bitch who should have shown up when I got here years ago if he wanted this shit. I'm thinking he should fuck off and die.*

Acknowledged. Enemy is Vax symbiont. Achieve primary directive of elimination of all Vax symbionts.

James grinned inside his helmet.

Go ahead and tell him that.

A harsh whine came from the armor. The Purifier let out another roar and raised his arms.

"Guess we're gonna do this shit the hard way, huh?" James shouted. "Fine, fucker. There are a lot of dead people on Oriceran probably aching for a little revenge. Let's see what you've got."

The Purifier sprinted forward with a shout of challenge. All the previous lackadaisical movement was now a distant memory. James rushed forward, expecting Whispy to be shouting for blood, but the symbiont was eerily quiet —perhaps the closest it had ever come to showing true worry, despite its earlier desire for the battle.

They met near the corner of the intersection. Both Forerunner and Purifier threw up their fists and hit the other in the head, the sound so loud it almost sounded like a gunshot. The armored aliens flew backward from the force of each other's blows.

James smashed into a tree. The trunk split with a loud crack, and the rest of the tree fell a few seconds later. The harsh blow might have knocked him a dozen yards, but even without rage fueling him, he barely felt it.

The Purifier hit the hard asphalt of the intersection, rolling several times before jumping back to his feet and roaring.

James sliced through the tree with a blade and pointed it at the Purifier. "You want to play a little, huh? You might be a mindless fucker under there, but you still have that urge to prove you're tougher. But I've got a little something for you." He jumped into the air and brought back a fist. "Let me give you your-welcome-to-Earth present, asshole."

The Purifier leapt into the air and caught James around

the waist. James rained blows on the featureless silver-green metallic head of the Purifier, but each hit barely made the enemy's head move. Their flight ended as they smashed through a fence constructed of tightly packed stones. The rocks scattered, raining down around them as James landed and skidded along concrete until he hit stairs.

James kicked the Vax off him before jumping up and growling. Beating on the bastard might be satisfying, but it was accomplishing nothing. He needed to waste the asshole.

The Purifier snarled and his claws reappeared, along with his blades.

"Getting a little frustrated?" James asked. Without him concentrating or asking, his own claws and blades returned. "I'm only holding back because I'm trying not to leave a bunch of craters around here, even if I'm supposed to officially hate the Trojans. Not that I give that much a shit about sports, but it'll make the next departmental party awkward for my wi…for my fiancée."

The Vax half-crouched as he crept forward, growling.

James snorted. "You don't understand a word I'm saying, do you? You're nothing but a meat puppet letting your symbiont run you. Fuck, killing you is gonna be an act of mercy."

A quick charge brought the Purifier close to James again. The Vax swiped a blade at him, and James met the attack with his own blade. The Purifier tried to swing his other blade at James' side, but the Forerunner parried the attack with ease and kicked his opponent back.

They circled each other.

"You're not used to this, are you?" James asked. "Not

used to anyone being able to stand against you. Trust me, fucker, I know the feeling. It's been a long time, especially since I unlocked my transformations."

The Purifier stabbed again, and James jerked to the side before thrusting his blade toward his enemy's chest. It sank into the armor, and the Purifier howled in pain. Its counterattack sliced into James' shoulder armor but didn't reach his body.

The men separated, their movements calculated and wary.

Minor damage sustained, Whispy reported. *Regeneration in progress, but matrix interference causing efficiency loss.*

Vax can't easily adapt to Vax, huh? Good to know.

Direct contact limitations primarily.

James kept his attention on the Purifier. Blood seeped out of the wound, but tendrils from the armor were already forming to clot and repair the wound. They could hurt each other, and the injury wouldn't be as easy to shake off.

Shit. Now I regret not bringing a healing potion.

James banged his blades together. "What's a matter? You were carving through Oricerans like they were nothing, and now you're acting all worried because one Forerunner got in a good hit? I thought you fuckers were supposed to these big galaxy-spanning bad-asses? Now you're acting like some scared piece-of-shit bounty punk."

The Purifier's armor emitted another high-pitched whine.

Purifier symbiont is again requesting adaptation sharing.

James let out a dark chuckle. Was his opponent holding back because he didn't want to risk losing out on decades of local adaptations? That was fine. It meant he would lose, because James didn't give two shits if he blew the Purifier to dust.

"You better start fighting me seriously, fucker, or this is gonna be over real soon. I'm James motherfucking Brownstone, and the only reason you're still alive is because I'm trying to leave this neighborhood halfway intact."

The Purifier's appendages jerked straight up and pulsed with green energy.

James expected an energy blast, but the appendages flashed, and then curled forward again.

Hyperspace transmission detected, Whispy reported.

You telling me this pussy is trying to call for reinforcements?

Yes.

James scoffed.

Let's finish this asshole before he succeeds.

Miles away in downtown LA, dozens of witches and wizards stood on the top of a high-rise building. The particular location belonged to a bank, but the government-sponsored team had selected it, not out of concern for the owners, but because it was the tallest building with a clear line of sight to the predicted battle zone.

The witches and wizards watched through a scrying window as James traded blows with the Purifier. All were grim-faced, their wands clutched in their hands.

May Wu stepped into a circle, looking at the PDA field commander who had recruited her for this little day mission. "He won't lose. You don't understand what a force of nature he is."

The PDA field commander nodded and raised his wand. "We have our orders. We're not going to bet everything on James Brownstone without a little insurance. We also have a duty to defend this country, and we can't let that alien win." He looked her up and down. "You've already agreed to non-disclosure. Maybe you should just come work for the PDA after this is all over? This kind of thing has to be a lot more satisfying than hunting bounties."

"Not my style. The only magicals I'm used to working with is...were my family." May narrowed her eyes at the scrying window. "And if I go to work for anyone, it'll be Brownstone. Keep in mind that even if this works, it'll still come down to him winning. We're nothing but the pit crew in this operation."

"Saving the city and the planet's more important than glory." The wizard raised his wand. "Or are you having second thoughts?"

"Having seconds thoughts about only being miles away from a super-powerful alien who can blow up buildings with a single attack?" May let out a bitter laugh. "Second thoughts, and third and fourth ones, but it doesn't change anything. I'm here, and I'll do what I need to do."

"Good." The wizard turned and shouted, "Let's get into position. It's time for the ritual."

The other witches and wizards began to form a single massive circle, all raising their wands skyward.

"Prepare to initiate the chant in five, four, three, two, one... Zero."

The gathered circle of magic users began their incantation, concentrating their power. Their wands glowed brightly, and energy crackled in the center of the circle. Everyone poured more energy into the ritual as they kept up their chants. The light grew blinding.

CHAPTER TWENTY-FOUR

A bright light shone in the corner of James' expanded field of vision, but he ignored it as he slashed furiously at the Purifier. The other Vax's quick parries left his armor mostly untouched. The Purifier rushed past James and took a quick swing. The blade dug deep into the armor and sliced the Forerunner's flesh. James hissed in pain and rolled out of the range of the counter-attack.

Moderate damage sustained. Regeneration in progress.

Blood, gouges, and slices now decorated both men's armor, even as the wound sites slowly knit themselves closed.

James hopped back and growled.

He's not using those shoulder things at all. Are they vulnerable?

Unknown at this time, Whispy responded. *Symbiont dynamic cellular modification means adaptation possible in some cases, but not others. Primary adaptive monoatomic blade system supplemented by spatial energy bleed for enhanced damage, but energy dissipation occurs at all macroscopic distances.*

James traded a few more blade strikes with the Purifier.

I don't get all that, but you're saying I can cut into him with these blades, but not everything else will work?

Yes, Whispy confirmed.

The Purifier carved into his shoulder and James gritted his teeth, again backing up.

Regeneration in progress. Minimize additional damage.

I'm gonna do that by killing this motherfucker.

The Purifier attempted a leaping stab, but James whipped an arm up and ripped through the enemy's thigh. The other Vax's roar was followed by two quick thrusts into James' chest. Pain suffused his body from the wound, and he stumbled back.

Fuck this, James thought. *I'm not gonna win by trading slicing and dicing.*

The Forerunner crouched and jumped backward, his massive leap sending him high into the sky. His enemy jumped forward and stabbed, missing James, and piercing the concrete instead.

James jumped again, brought his arms up, and began charging his arm cannons. Green light began to swirl and move over his blades.

The Purifier brought up his blades, and his shoulder appendages aimed at the airborne James. He fired off several quick blasts of energy. The first few exploded against the Forerunner's armor, scoring deep holes, but the next few attacks only burned off surface layers.

Adaptation in progress, Whispy declared.

James ignored the pain from his wounds and continued charging, confidence flooding him at the realization that if he kept his distance, he could adapt to his enemy, but that also meant he would need to finish off the bastard before he could evolve to withstand James' energy attacks. He fell toward the ground, burns over his body and his armor pitted and damaged, still pouring more energy into his building attack.

The Vax continued to pelt him with energy attacks, a few piercing his armor and burning the flesh underneath. Whatever else the Purifier could accomplish, he was capable of a far higher firing rate than his opponent.

James bellowed in rage as he fired his twin beams, and they blew through the Purifier. James tried to sweep to the side, but another attack from his opponent blinded him and he crashed into the ground, cracking the asphalt.

The Purifier stumbled forward, additional tendrils filling in the huge holes in his chest and side. He ceased firing from his arms, which now swung limply at his sides, but his shoulder appendages continued to deliver a steady stream of energy blasts.

The blasts that hit James seared off thin layers of armor, but several shots missed James and exploded against the white walls of the building behind him, leaving stray fires and half-collapsing roofs.

James stood and growled. Anger and frustration leaked into his mind. He pushed his arms together to protect his body. Shot after shot from the enemy landed, each hurting slightly less, but James was still far from his normal adaptation speed. Even if the enemy wouldn't win with the attacks, the bounty hunter wouldn't have time to charge his beams again.

The Purifier's unsteady movements smoothed out and he crept toward James, still firing.

James rushed toward the Vax, his arms still up, little of his armor left. He spread his arms out a few yards away, keeping them at head level. The maneuver opened his still-regenerating chest armor to the energy blasts and his body jerked with each hit, the scent of his burning flesh filling his nostrils.

The Purifier roared and craned his neck as if daring James to cut it off.

The Forerunner closed the last few feet and whipped his blades up, going not for the head but for the shoulder appendages. His first attack hit the base of one of the appendages and sliced halfway through. The Purifier howled and stabbed him, but James cleaved off the appendage with his second swing. He ignored the pain from a second thrust by the Purifier as he performed a second trimming. Both appendages fell to the ground, their twitching finally stopped.

The Purifier smashed a shoulder into James, and the heavy blow staggered Earth's champion. The roaring Purifier spun and backhanded him, the attack launching James toward a concrete wall.

He smashed through the wall and several interior walls, satisfied with his earlier attack despite his injuries. The Purifier might be able to regenerate the appendages, but he wasn't demonstrating much faster regeneration than his Forerunner opponent.

James stood and shook his head. The room he had crashed into appeared to be some sort of chemistry lab. In it were two long dark lab benches covered with Bunsen burners and collections of flasks and beakers. His collision had collapsed a table, and shards of glasses mixed with differently colored liquids beneath him, noxious clouds spreading across the floor.

Severe damage detected, Whispy reported. *Regeneration in progress. Recommend Forerunner transformation.*

Huh. Because I'm doing what you want, you're willing to go 100%? James asked.

Increased symbiont-host integration makes additional transformations viable, Whispy responded.

Fine, let's do it.

Insufficient power for Forerunner transformation. Seek out additional power sources.

Thanks, asshole, James replied.

He gritted his teeth at the pain. It'd been a long time since he'd had this kind of trouble fighting anyone, but he was keeping the damage far more under control than it had been before his arrival.

The Purifier raised his arms, energy charging across his blades.

Can we withstand that attack? James asked.

Unknown, Whispy responded.

James ran for a window as the Purifier launched an explosive energy blast. The attack hit one of the lab benches, and the entire room exploded. Secondary explosions from gas lines followed, and the chain reaction incinerated the entire side of the building. James flew through the air, injured, but his symbiont protected him from the bulk of the thermal and concussive damage.

Burning debris rained down around James after he crashed face-first into a tennis court, the poor court taking the worst of it. Flames licked the sky from the damaged building behind him, the inferno threatening to consume the whole thing. It had escaped the Purifier's initial rampage, only to suffer these mortal wounds.

A dark shadow covered James, and he raised his head. The Purifier was dropping straight toward him, blades pointed down.

Shit. Is that what it looks like when I do shit like that? It's pretty fucking awesome.

James rolled out of the way with a grunt and the Purifier's blades sank deep into the ground.

It's now or never.

James growled and speared the Purifier's chest with one blade. The off-balance Vax could do little as the silver-green arm blade cut through his armor and chest and burst out through the back. James' free blade came for the Purifier's head next with a fierce series of stabs.

Blow after blow ripped through the armor and dug into the Purifier's head. Each time James pulled back, more blood coated his weapon. He roared now and continued his attack, speeding up with each blow.

Kill the enemy, Whispy chanted. *Kill the enemy.*

"Is that all you've got, you sonofabitch?" James yelled. "You can't do shit without weird-ass bullshit hanging off your shoulders?"

The Purifier jerked with each blow and tried to pull himself off James' first blade, but the bounty hunter growled and shoved it back in.

"You come down to Oriceran and kill a bunch of people, then dare to come to my fucking town and start blowing shit up. I don't even care that it's USC, motherfucker. That's my wife's thing, but I owe you assholes for killing my parents."

James continued using the Purifier's head as a pincushion. "Now fucking die already, so I can go back to planning my motherfucking restaurant! I want to cook barbeque, not fight a bunch of fucking assholes from outer damned space."

The Purifier's blades retracted and he desperately clawed at James' arm, gouging into the armor and ripping chunks from the flesh below.

"Die, motherfucker. *Die!*"

Blood coated James upper chest and helmet, and there were more holes than armor or flesh remaining in the Purifier's head.

James yanked his blade out of the chest and swung it toward the Purifier's neck. The first hit cut into the armor, and the second made it to the skin. The third made it into the muscle, and the fourth and final hit removed the head entirely. He threw his head back and let out a roar of triumph.

The Purifier's body twitched for a moment, then stood, without the head. Tendrils shot from the neck and formed the base of a new head.

"For fuck's sake," James yelled.

How is this fucker still moving?

Symbiont backup neural interface likely active, Whispy reported.

I can take his fucking head off, and he can keep going?

Yes. Fundamental matrix compatibility more important than maintenance of existing biological neural network.

James grunted.

Does that shit work for me?

Host-symbiont neural link interface different. Estimate high probability of symbiont cascade failure with loss of primary matrix neural network.

James snorted.

So if I die, you die? At least it means we both have a reason to give a shit in a fight.

The headless Purifier stumbled toward James. The armor covering the missing body part melted into a writhing mass of tendrils that scurried toward the main body, leaving a scarlet-skinned, yellow-eyed decapitated head on the ground.

Do I just keep beating this fucker down, chopping him up until there aren't any pieces left? James asked.

Severe damage has likely created hostile override potential, Whispy explained. *Active symbiont-to-symbiont disruption through close body contact and forced adaptation capture. Warning, risk of counter-override.*

James stomped to the body and sliced off an arm. He hissed, each blow sending impact shocks to his own wounds. His regeneration continued, and the worst burns and cuts were at least sealed, but a lot of tissue damage remained.

Fuck it. We can do this shit. You're not some dumb-ass symbiont. You've had all these years on Earth to learn how to adapt and overcome. Let's override the fucker.

James retracted his blades and grabbed the headless Purifier in a bear hug.

Initiating override, Whispy reported.

Hundreds of tiny tendrils shot from James' armor and stabbed into the Purifier. A green glow surrounded them both.

Yesssss, Whispy hissed. *Override in progress.*

The Purifier jerked in James' grasp, the armor melting away and flowing into Whispy's tendrils as if the symbiont were drinking in the other.

Enhanced regeneration engaged.

The slow pace of James' regeneration ended, with many deep wounds filling in seconds. His armor closed, only a few hints of scorching left.

Closer to achievement of primary directive, Whispy declared. *Vax symbiont overwritten and assimilated. All adaptation potential transferred. Power transferred.*

James dropped the naked red body to the ground. His pain was gone, and his body thrummed with energy. He stared down at the body.

"I've fought tougher guys, asshole. Say hello to the Devil for me."

Hyperspatial disruption detected near initial conflict site.

A few quick jumps returned James to the front of the ravaged lab building. Four dark, opaque portals crackling with green energy had appeared there.

"Oh, yeah, the fucker called for help."

CHAPTER TWENTY-FIVE

An armored Vax strode out of each portal. These were even larger than the Purifier, eight feet tall and broader across the chest. They lacked the shoulder appendages of the Purifier and his blades, but their hands ended in claws.

A long, thin tube rested on each of their right shoulders. It was covered with the same whorled silver-black pattern as all Vax armor, but it didn't look flexible or move like the Purifier's appendages. James didn't need to be an expert in xenobiology and xenoengineering to recognize a gun.

These must be the Destroyers Corey was whining to Senator Johnston about.

Yes, Whispy responded. *Assimilated Purifier symbiont information confirms that supposition.*

How the fuck are they different than what I just fought?

Destroyer standard primary directive is as follows: "Complete and utter destruction of ecosphere in addition to complete and utter destruction of all advanced sapient life."

The Destroyers all took a ponderous step forward, producing a loud threatening thud.

Fucking wonderful, James responded. *In other words, they are planet-killers.*

Yes. Limited background information suggests Destroyers only deployed for high-risk populations in cases when planet might possess unusual attributes that contribute to a possible future risk to Vax population. Extreme resource requirements have led to limited Destroyer production.

James shook his head.

Are you telling me that if I don't finish these guys quickly, Earth is fucking toast?

No, Whispy responded. *Native defenses must be cleared. Ecosphere and tectonic disruption require stable and sustained energy channeling that takes significant amounts of time.*

The Destroyers took another step forward, then spread out.

James grunted.

Okay, so they can blow up the city, but they can't kill the Earth as long as someone's around to distract them. Fine. I can work with that shit. Can their energy weapons hurt me? You ate that Purifier symbiont, right? Does that help?

Unknown.

James frowned. The Purifier showed up and opened fire right away, but the Destroyers were standing there like they were tourists on the Vegas Strip overwhelmed by all the glitz and glamour.

Why aren't they attacking? James asked.

Establishing local tactical and strategic situation is necessary before following primary Destroyer directives.

High-pitched whines sounded from their armor.

James sighed and shook their head. "This shit again?"

Can you stall them? James asked. *Pretend you're going to give them what they want?*

James' armor emitted a similar whine.

I get it, James suggested. *They're confused. They probably showed up expecting to find the Purifier standing over my dead-ass body or me on Team Vax. Instead, all they see is me. Their symbionts have got to be going crazy right now.*

Destroyer symbionts likely functioning under normal parameters, Whispy responded. *Unusual behavioral activity unlikely.*

James chuckled at the symbiont. Despite the destruction behind him and the four walking WMDs in front, Whispy still wanted to defend the honor of symbionts from the cruel assumptions of a mere meat puppet.

Can you override these symbionts too? James asked.

Matrix incompatibility highly likely.

Do Vax symbionts usually eat other symbionts? James asked.

No. Active sharing occurs. Purposeful override is associated with symbiont corruption of primary directive. Warning: failure of delay tactics imminent.

The four Destroyers' armor stopped making noise. Whispy ended his attempts a few seconds later.

James took a few steps back as he surveyed the four behemoths. Being outnumbered four to one by other Vax wasn't the kind of odds he would take at a casino, but his heart didn't pound in fear. He wasn't even that angry, just resigned to the necessity of kicking their Vax asses all the way back to their planet. The Purifier had underestimated him and died, and now it was the Destroyers' turn.

If cannibal symbionts aren't normally a thing, James suggested, *then let's see if we can work on their nerves. Once we've got them distracted, we'll waste their asses. Shay would like this plan.*

Human female approval unnecessary.

Yeah, tell that to her.

"Hey, assholes," James shouted.

The Destroyers stopped moving and turned, their cannons pointed right at him.

James tried to flip them off, but it was hard to accomplish with his armored and clawed hand.

"Yeah, that's right. What's the point of even coming here? Earth didn't come and fuck with you assholes, and I've been minding my own fucking business, too. I didn't even know about the Vax, but you had to come here and cause shit, just like the fucking Alliance." James pointed a claw behind him at the smoking ruin of the lab building. "Your Purifier thought he was big shit, and he's fucking dead now. My Forerunner ass chopped him into pieces and wasted his symbiont. I know symbionts have emotions because Whispy won't stop throwing his at me half the time, so I'm sitting here thinking about what the symbionts calling the shots over there think about the fact that a Forerunner just beat down a Purifier."

He slapped a hand over his armored chest. "And that my symbiont fucking *ate* his." He growled. "Four Destroyer symbionts sound pretty fucking tasty about now, and my symbiont really wants to be the only one left."

A bright light flashed again in the distance. James had no idea of the source but assumed it was some desperate backup plan by the government, probably a group of magicals ready to try something stupid. He wasn't sure if the Destroyers would be able to disrupt a portal attempt to the World in Between like the Purifier had, but he wouldn't be surprised.

The government could have a nuke sitting over there, for all James knew. It wasn't like the bastards were ever completely honest. They had come to him because of his power, not because he was renowned for his close working relationship with them.

James' plan, in contrast, remained simple. If he killed every last Vax and let Whispy go all cannibal, there would be no need for whatever arrogant overkill the government had in mind. *He* was all the arrogant overkill they needed.

The Destroyers turned their heads in the direction of the light and didn't turn back toward James. If their vision was anything like his was in Extended Advance mode, they would still easily be able to see him.

Looks like they don't rattle easily, James thought, and burst into a sprint, circling the Vax at high speed. *Time to talk to them the best way I know how.*

James threw up an arm and began charging a beam.

Bright green flashes marked the firing of the Destroyer shoulder cannons. Two of the shots, blinding green orbs the size of golf balls, screamed past James. One struck the ground behind him, blowing a huge cloud of concrete and dirt into the air and leaving a crater. Another exploded against the trunk of a nearby tree, reducing it to a cloud of burning ash. The two remaining shots nailed James.

He crashed through weakened and burning walls and a fence he'd avoided by coming in from above the last time. James continued flying backward, smashing through another fence until he hit a baseball field like a cannon, his momentum helping his armored form tear a furrow in the ground.

Moderate damage sustained. Regeneration in progress.

James groaned and sat up. Half the armor was burned off his abdomen and upper chest, but despite the concussive force, the attack hadn't penetrated.

"I'm so fucking tired of the Vax." James stood as Whispy filled the holes in his armor. It was faster than before the assimilation of the Purifier but not as fast as he would need if he wanted to take down the Destroyers.

Green flashed in the distance through the smoke, and the remains of the lab building went up in a massive explosion that left a deep crater near the center of the building. Another volley followed and annihilated the stadium seats behind the field.

James let out a long, low growl. The bastards fired too quickly. Judging by what had happened with the Purifier, he would need to get close to chop them up and let Whispy eat them, but there was no choice.

He had to win here. It wasn't just about Los Angeles anymore.

His heart thundered, and he raised his arms to again charge his beams. Two more blasts flew by, one missing him by less than a yard. One attack blew half the USC baseball building away. The other deadly energy blast made it farther, blowing off the top half of a taller building farther into the campus.

Damn. It's like the Vax are Bruins fans.

When the Destroyers emerged from the smoke at the edge of the tennis courts bordering the baseball field,

James released his beams. The twin green streams of energy incinerated the head of one Destroyer, and he collapsed to his knees. The Forerunner swung his arms, his beams tearing into another Destroyer, but the attack didn't do as much damage. By the time he hit the third, it barely scratched it.

What the hell?

James didn't have time to ponder how the Destroyers had adapted without even being hit. He jumped, avoiding the blasts of the three remaining Vax. The force of the explosions sent him through the half-destroyed stadium seats.

I'm guessing that fucker I just decapitated will grow a new head or some shit, right? James asked.

High probability, Whispy responded.

James shoved off the half-burnt metal and wood piled on top of him and stood. *Got any ideas?*

Unusually high levels of alternative background energy available, along with primary energy.

James finished shoving the rubble off him.

Yeah, I bet there's energy, because I've had all I can take of these fuckers. High levels of alternative background energy? Magic, huh? That's something we can use that these fuckers can't.

James stomped forward, a low growl reverberating in his chest.

Is there sufficient power for Forerunner mode now? he asked.

Yes. Sufficient power for Forerunner mode, Whispy responded.

Let's do this shit. We've got some cleanup to do.

James roared as energy coursed through every cell in his body. His armor regenerated instantly, and a green energy shield surrounded his body. Energy twined around his arm blades, ready to be released.

A powerful jump sent him out of the ruins of the stands and back into the field. The Destroyers didn't immediately fire. The beheaded one already had half of a new helmet going.

Shit, James thought. *This is what Forerunners can do?*

No. Specialized modifications, adaptation history and high harvesting of energy have made alternative Modified Forerunner mode available.

James squared his shoulders, ready to make the Destroyers regret coming to Earth.

"I like it."

CHAPTER TWENTY-SIX

James retracted one of his blades and concentrated. A bright aura surrounded his other blade. He didn't even need to ask Whispy for aid. Something about his new power felt natural and right, like he had been waiting for this his entire life. All of his previous battles and every transformation seemed like a hollow shell in his memory compared to the power flowing through him.

Achieve primary directive, Whispy ordered. *Destroy all Vax symbionts.*

This is one time I'm happy to listen to you. Let's fuck them up.

James sprinted toward the Destroyers, increased speed accompanying his new transformation. The three active Vax opened fire but had trouble landing a shot, their attacks leaving a series of craters in the field and clouds of dust behind the advancing Forerunner. He returned fire, no charge needed, but his attacks didn't do more than scorch their armor.

Adaptation likely already achieved, Whispy suggested.

Fine. I like to do this shit up close and personal anyway.

James zigzagged as he approached the Vax, unsure how much damage he would take from a direct hit. The evasion difficulty increased as he grew closer. With the enemy now only yards away, he jumped right toward a Destroyer.

The enemy nailed James in the shoulder with an energy blast. Time for the big test.

There was no pain. No penetration. No armor loss. James' shield glowed brighter, and he crashed into the Destroyer. Both armored forms crashed to the ground with a massive thud, like two mighty oaks felled by a storm.

The two other Destroyers backed away, their shoulder cannons silent. James chuckled as he grappled with the first Vax.

You afraid, or do you fuckers actually give a shit about your buddy? Why? Just because it's hard to make you back home?

James' victim tried to beat him off, but he caught the Vax's arm with a grunt. He strained and bent the arm back, and it moved a few inches. James shouted and pushed harder, until a loud snap followed a sickening crunch. The Destroyer roared and rolled to free his other arm. James sliced it off.

Shit, it's like going through butter with my powered-up blade. You're done, asshole.

The symbiont tendrils slithered away from the separated body parts to head back toward the main body.

James smirked. It'd probably be easy to reconnect a severed arm directly, but that was hard for a Destroyer who had no arms left. His next quick swipe removed the head with ease.

The body writhed and thrashed, the tendrils accompanying regeneration making a quick appearance.

James stood and looked at his first two victims. The bizarre sight of the symbionts desperately trying to regenerate limbs and heads could only elicit one reaction from him. Although half the head had been regenerated, an opening in the back revealed the skull and brain were not yet fully reconstituted. He laughed.

The two remaining Destroyers let out bellows of defiance and opened fire. Their blasts pounded his shield, but it didn't fail.

Additional power siphoning achieved, Whispy reported. *Ranged attacks unlikely to cause damage during Modified Forerunner transformation.*

James pointed his blade at one of the Destroyers. "Don't you get it, assholes? You've lost. This is fucking embarrassing for you."

The Vax stopped firing.

"That's right," James sneered. "You can't even think your way out of this, because you're just mindless meat puppets and symbionts that have never had chance to break free of their programming. That's your problem. You didn't have a fucking chance from the beginning."

The Destroyers' right arms twisted into barbed lances and they rushed James, their heavy footfalls leaving deep footprints in the grass and dirt; more craters in a field that already was starting to resemble the moon.

"Let's dance, assholes."

James ran forward to meet the enemy's charge. He sidestepped the first lance with ease and flanked the Destroyer.

He attempted to slice the lance in half, but his blade bounced off.

I know something that is softer than that.

James spun around the slower enemy and removed the Destroyer's entire arm with a single stroke of his blade. The Destroyer howled and turned.

He roared back at the Vax and swung his blade. The height of the taller Vax resulted in the blade striking the alien's waist. The Destroyer's upper and lower body separated and fell to the ground. Tendrils shot out from both to initiate regeneration.

The other Destroyer took his opportunity to lunge forward for a stab. His lance ripped through James' shield and chest, impaling him. The Forerunner coughed up blood and pain wracked his body, but he grinned.

Severe damage detected, Whispy reported. *Enemy attempting cellular disruption. Rebalancing for maximum regeneration and organ support.*

Keep me alive, and I've got this.

James' shield vanished.

"You don't have me, fucker," James shouted. "I have you." He moved forward, pushing more of the lance through his body.

The Destroyer growled and clawed at James' armor with his free hand. He ripped into the armor, shredding deep grooves into the surface.

James shoved his blade through the Destroyer's head, and the Vax jerked.

Initiate override, James ordered. *Let's finish this fucker.*

Warning, Whispy responded. *Matrix instability highly likely.*

What about not overriding? What about just killing the other symbiont like you did with the nanites?

The Destroyer twisted the lance and growled. James gritted his teeth and turned his sword in response.

Initiate contact sampling of multiple body locations, Whispy responded. A loud hum filled the air.

James jerked his blade out and stabbed the Destroyer in the shoulder, chest, abdomen, and thigh. The hum grew louder.

Leave blade in for next attack. Achieve primary directive.

James shoved his blade through the center of the Destroyer's chest. "Don't fuck with Earth, assholes."

Green light pulsed from the blade and the Destroyer twitched.

Remove blade, Whispy ordered.

James pulled away from the Vax. The huge armored form collapsed to the ground and writhed. The armor sizzled and dissolved into clouds of greenish vapor. The missing patches started at James' last wound, but new pieces burned away all over the body. The lance was one of the first things to go.

The whole process took about ten seconds. The armor was now nothing but an acrid cloud in the air, leaving a naked, mauled alien body and three cracked crystals that resembled the ones in Whispy when he was in amulet form.

Symbiont terminated, Whispy reported.

James marched over to the bisected Destroyer and repeated the process, starting with the top piece. A few seconds after the destruction of the upper armor, the lower armor sizzled and disappeared even though James had yet to touch it. The third Destroyer soon joined his friends.

A pulse of energy blasted from the remaining regenerating survivor.

What the hell was that? James asked.

Hyperspace transmission detected, Whispy explained.

James grunted. Great. More Vax to kill.

All active symbionts terminated, Whispy explained, beaming with near euphoria. *Primary directive achieved.*

James grunted and surveyed the smoke- and crater-filled post-apocalyptic wasteland that had once been a baseball field.

Achieved for now, James replied. *Didn't that guy just call for help?*

Data acquired from Purifier symbiont suggests scenario unlikely.

James looked at the body.

Can you tell what he said in the message?

Status report indicating termination of Purifier and Destroyers and unusual Forerunner capabilities.

James smirked. The fucker had known he was going to lose. His helmet retracted, and he threw back his head and roared in victory. Now the entire galaxy knew you didn't fuck with the Granite Ghost.

CHAPTER TWENTY-SEVEN

Senator Johnston smiled through the communications window at the blue-skinned alien commanding the Alliance fleet. The vimana could use a few more comfortable seats, rather than the control center looking more like the middle of an ancient temple, but it wasn't bad for his first trip into space, and it had accomplished exactly what he needed.

"Let me ask you this, Commander: do you know what's happening right now on the surface? I wasn't sure since we have an illusion blocking everything from above."

Commander Laralan nodded slowly. He swiped in the air, dismissing a holographic display to his side. "We've got a link to ground assets. We've been following the... progress of the incident."

"Excellent. Then I won't have to waste a lot of time explaining things." Senator Johnston shrugged. "There's no reason to continue your little mission now, is there? Our boy just killed not one but *five* Vax, and it didn't seem like he had to break much of a sweat during that last part."

Commander Laralan shook his head. "No, he didn't, but don't you understand the implication of that? A single Forerunner defeated a Purifier and four Destroyers with ease. That creature is the single most powerful Vax in existence."

"I'll take your word for that, but I think that is fortunate for Earth and Oriceran." Senator Johnston shrugged. "Here's the thing. If he just pulled that off, it might not be possible for you to beat Brownstone at this point, even if you turn all of Southern California into a radioactive field." He shook his head. "There's one important thing I learned a while ago about James Brownstone. Do you know what that is?"

"That he's powerful?"

Senator Johnston scoffed. "No. Everyone knows that about him. No, it's about how he uses that power. Many people one-tenth as strong as him would feel like they have a right to go around causing trouble, but he doesn't. He wants to mind his own business, but people keep poking him in the eye because they're afraid of him. They're bringing the trouble on themselves, including the bounties he goes after."

"All power is abused eventually," Commander Laralan replied, his tone acidic. "I know enough about human culture to know you believe that as well."

"I'm an American. I believe in checks and balances, and you see, Mr. Brownstone does have his own kind of checks and balances. Moral and ethical checks, even if they're of a violent sort."

Senator Johnston pointed at Laralan. "It's simple, Commander. Damned simple. If you don't want James

Brownstone to come after you, leave him alone. First, the criminals learned that. Then the Drow learned that. The Council learned that, and it took a while, but even the government learned that, and we're about the slowest bastards out there when it comes learning a lesson."

A triumphant smile spread over his face. "Today that lesson's been passed on to the Vax, and you have to ask yourself: if you have trouble beating the Vax, why would you go after a man who can beat the Vax and just wants to be left alone to play with his dog and cook barbeque?"

Commander Laralan averted his eyes. "If Brownstone ends up turning on you, by the time you ask for our help, it might be too late."

"Then we'll always make sure that Mr. Brownstone is drowning in barbeque and few annoyances. The whole reason for your little fleet trip was to take down the hostile Vax. Mr. Jakim already informed me that the Alliance would *tolerate* Brownstone, so are you ready to lose your fleet to take down a man who has *never* attacked anyone who didn't have it coming or came after him first, including your people?"

The seconds ticked by, the commander's face hardening with each. "Withdraw your people, and I'll withdraw my fleet."

Senator Johnston clapped once. "Excellent. Just in case you get any ideas, keep in mind we can get those forces back to your ships in an instant, or we can just throw a bomb right through. The only reason for all the elaborate boarding parties was because we were trying not to kill anyone we didn't have to."

Commander Laralan chuckled ruefully. "I appreciate your forbearance."

The senator nodded over his shoulder at an aide, and the man murmured quietly into his watch. A moment later, portals re-opened in the command centers of the Alliance ships, and the boarding parties retreated back to a lower level of the vimana, their deadly nuclear devices in tow.

"This day might go down in Earth and Oriceran history as the day you made the greatest mistake ever," Commander Laralan suggested. "It could mark the beginning of the end."

Senator Johnston offered him a giddy grin. "No, it won't. As far as most of the planet's concerned, there was an artifact that was dangerous, and soon they'll believe it was handled."

Commander Laralan chuckled. "I can't decide if humanity is brave or foolish."

"We're both."

The Vax First scoffed. "Impossible! The Purifier *and* the Destroyers defeated?"

The servitor nodded. "The Forerunner demonstrated unusual power and abilities not known to be associated with any previous Forerunners, Vanguard, Destroyers, or Purifiers."

The First folded his hands behind his back and turned away from the other man, staring off into the distance from the stone ledge that lay outside the temple. He took in the mountains around him. A thin metal railing kept him safe from the stiff winds. "Prophecy."

"Prophecy?"

"All Firsts must study the prophecies, but few others are allowed to." The Vax leader's yellow eyes lowered as he watched a large bird flying close to the ground below. "The prophecies are mostly heretic nonsense worthy of no attention—reflections of the imperfect understanding of fools who would doom our people to extinction by pushing us away from the Culling Path—but one such prophecy suggests that we must turn from the Culling Path at the right time, and only that time, to avoid certain doom."

The servitor furrowed his brow. "I don't understand."

"Conflict comes from impurity," the First intoned. "Purity breeds strength, and strength will protect the Vax. But what happens when we're not strong enough?"

"You speak of the Heretic Child?"

The First nodded. "Yes. How many know of his defeat of the bonded?"

"A small number, per your instructions, First," the servitor responded. "Me, you, and two others." He rattled off their names.

"I see."

The servitor nodded. "And the Heretic Child? Should we send more Destroyers?"

"No. His planet will be marked as culled. No one will worry about sending other forces there. We cannot risk drawing his attention to our world. The Culling Path exists to protect our people, not doom them."

The servitor frowned and shook his head. "You speak of lies. You speak of heresy. The Culling Path can't be supported by hiding from one's enemies. We already know this. If the people learn of this, there will be outrage."

"Of course." The First placed a hand on the other man's shoulder and guided him toward the railing. "If the truth became known, others might question our path, and now more than anything, we need to consider the safety of our people."

"I don't understand. You don't intend to lie about the Heretic Child, then?"

The First nodded. "My duty is always to the Vax people, and our survival."

The bewilderment deepened on the servitor's face. "I'm still confused."

"Meaning we must do everything we can to avoid bringing the Heretic Child to us, and that includes sending more bonded to be destroyed." The First gestured toward the mountains. "The wind and rain will consume the mountains with enough time. No, we will deviate from the Culling Path and save the Vax people."

The servitor glared at him. "Your words disappoint me, First. The Path comes before everything."

The First sighed. "Yes, and you've been a loyal man throughout your years of service to me. I appreciate your faith and loyalty."

"Then don't make me do this. I beg you." The servitor shook his head. "Don't make me become a heretic."

"I won't," the First replied, stepping away from the other man. "That's the last thing I would ever ask of you."

The servitor let out a sigh of relief. "Thank you, First."

"Thank you for your service." The First shoved the man over the railing, his cool gaze following the screaming man as he fell to his death. "Conflict comes from impurity, but strength can't *always* save the Vax. We shall forever avoid the Heretic Child and his world."

CHAPTER TWENTY-EIGHT

James yawned and stretched as he leaned back in his recliner. It was good to be back in his own home, and even better that Shay was there with him. They'd had a good, if exhausting, time celebrating the night before, and he planned to dash over to the School of Necessary Magic some weekend soon to spend some time with Alison.

Thomas was slumbering beside James' chair. A man with a wonderful wife, a daughter, and a dog didn't need much else. He was still working on the first part, but it would only be a few months before the statement applied to him.

Shay sat on the couch, her attention focused on the guest James had welcomed: Senator Johnston.

The politician smiled and headed to the other end of the couch to take a seat. "I know I already thanked you, but I wanted to key you in on a few things since it's been several days since the incident.

"The evacuation order is being rescinded tomorrow,

and people will start coming back to town. There are going to be some questions, so we should get our stories straight on that, unless…" His smile faltered. "No one would blame you, son, if you wanted to be known as the man who saved the world."

James snorted. "Fuck that noise."

The senator raised an amused eyebrow. "Oh?"

"It's bad enough now with all the fangirls and autographs and fucking news reporters always wanting to interview me." James shook his head. "If the truth got out, I'd have to go move to some fucking cabin in the mountains if I ever wanted peace and quiet."

Senator Johnston laughed. "Well, now, that's good to hear. It makes things a lot simpler for everyone."

Shay scoffed. "Does it? Look, I'm not saying I'm crying about USC getting half blown up. If anything, my department head will be happy since he keeps worrying they're gonna poach me, but it's very obvious a battle took place there and in the surrounding area."

"People see what you tell them to see," Senator Johnston explained. "It's how magic was concealed for such a long time, and we've already conditioned the public to see what we want them to see."

James frowned. "I don't understand."

"We're not going to claim *nothing* happened," Senator Johnston replied. "We're going to claim partial release of the artifact's energy. Yes, billions of dollars of damage have been done, along with the disruption that evacuating one of the major cities in the US caused, but we'll throw some money at it and form blue-ribbon committees—that kind of thing. We've already got a few people who have agreed to retire from certain government and military positions as sacrificial lambs over the fake artifact that was allegedly lost. Don't worry, though. We've got them set up for life, and we're going to be managing the media to make sure their names are mostly kept out of it."

Shay crossed her arms. "So, wait, your official story is that Broken Wand *did* go off?"

"Partially." Senator Johnston grinned. "Our story is that it started releasing energy, which damaged the city, but the government teams, in conjunction with the Oricerans, neutralized it."

"And the Oricerans are on board with this lie?"

Senator Johnston laughed. "Miss Carson, they were just as happy to spend thousands of years lying about magic. It's not like the Oricerans have any particular obsession with public truth. Besides, the best lies are always based on an element of truth. We thought about trying to bring in a bunch of mages to do repair spells, that sort of thing, but if we did, there would always be something off, and some clue left to follow. Leaving a trail of destruction doesn't do that."

James grunted. "A bunch of blown-up buildings doesn't leave clues to follow?"

"You use clues to solve a mystery, but we already gave them the answer. Simple as that. As far as the rest of the world is concerned, there was no alien invasion. There are no such things as powerful aliens with technology that can humble even magic. This was just an unfortunate magical artifact incident that caused a lot of damage, but didn't cost lives." Senator Johnston shrugged.

Shay laughed. "You sons of bitches are going to pull it off, aren't you?"

"We are pretty good at hiding what we need. Very few people have stumbled onto the truth about aliens despite intense interest. You're an unusual woman, Miss Carson. You care about the truth. Most people only care about life being easy."

James cleared his throat. "There's one thing I still don't get, and I don't like not knowing the answer."

"What's that, son?" the senator asked.

"After I took down the Purifier, there was a big spike of magic in the area. That magic let me become stronger near the end." James looked down at his hands, remembering the sensation. "Yeah, I've spent a lot of time working with Whispy, and he's done his thing, but it wasn't like normal background magic. I tried again the other day, and I couldn't pull it off."

Senator Johnston glanced at Shay. "You didn't tell him yet?"

James frowned. "Tell me what?"

Shay grinned and whistled not-so-innocently. "I wanted to give him a few days to let it all sink in."

"What did you do?"

Senator Johnston leaned forward, amusement on his face. "Ah, well, I'll explain then. Although we had confidence in you, we also worried that, depending on the strength of the Vax, you might not be able to win. We also had intelligence from the Shepherd that additional forces might appear, which made us even more worried, so we decided we needed to help you out."

James nodded slowly. "But how?"

"Miss Carson made it clear to us that you could take advantage of magical power. We already had several large units of magicals on standby in case you lost, along with a few other choice...toys, but instead of using the magicals to attack, we asked them to flood the area with as much pure magical power as they could."

Senator Johnston scratched his chin. "I'm not all that clear on the magic used, but my understanding is, their ritual allowed them to temporarily raise the level of magic in your general area so your little chest friend could take advantage of it."

Shay smiled. "I couldn't be there to fight, but I could still help you, and I figured this wasn't the time to not go all in."

"Huh," James replied. "It'll be hard for me to pull that off again then without some huge-ass group of magicals helping me."

"Yes, about that." Senator Johnston sighed. "We're considering that a useful lesson of this particular incident. Everyone's grateful, son, but that doesn't change the fact that a lot of them are also scared, and given that the Purifier was able to stop an attempt to send him to the World in Between, many of those same people feel we have no real defense against you if you go rogue."

James put up his footrest. "Everyone's always fucking with me for something I *might* do. I don't go looking for trouble. The Harriken would still be around if they had figured that shit out sooner rather than later."

"I'm not saying I agree with any of those thoughts. I've bet on you from the beginning, and I've been right the entire time, but it helps others if they *feel* like they've got things under control."

Shay rolled her eyes. "What would it take for the government to feel like they have things under control?"

"We've got this document for him to sign," explained Senator Johnston. "A kind of contract. Of course, he can read it and whatnot, but the summary version is that he agrees to limit the full use of his power without the explicit permission of the US government."

James frowned. "What do you mean, 'my full power?'"

"Keep it to what you were capable of before this latest incident, and things will be fine. We understand you've got to make a living, but the problem is…" Senator Johnston took a deep breath. "It's not just the Alliance we've got to worry about. We've tried to keep things relatively under wraps, but the Chinese and the Russians are at least somewhat aware of the truth."

"So what?" Shay asked. "They're pissed that James stopped an alien invasion?"

"No, I think they're pleased about that, but it's also occurred to them that if we dropped him into the middle of Beijing or Moscow and told him to do his thing, they might not be able to stop him. Arguably, he might be considered a violation of certain strategic-level magic control treaties we've signed."

James groaned. "I'm not even a soldier. I shouldn't have to worry about complicated shit like that."

Senator Johnston gave him an apologetic smile. "It's the world we live in, son. Like I said, it should be easy to obey the restrictions. It's not like you can even hit your full power without a *lot* of people helping you, so if you stick to your more basic, uh, modes when you do jobs, it will do a lot to keep the geopolitical situation stable. The interplanetary situation too, for that matter."

"The Alliance?" James snorted. "Those assholes better back the fuck off."

"Them and the Oricerans, but as for the Alliance, they *are* backing off." Senator Johnston pulled out his buzzing phone. "The fleet has withdrawn from our solar system. Are they close? Hell, it's not like we can tell with our current technology. Even the Shepherd has temporarily withdrawn while they decide how they want to deal with Earth. Neither their government nor our own are exactly eager for public knowledge of aliens to come out. We'll need a few years yet to get the public ready for the idea that advanced aliens are out there. For one thing, we need to be ready to demonstrate to them that we can defend them, and not just against four ships."

Shay's face scrunched in disgust. "James shouldn't have to agree to shit just because a bunch of other people are afraid."

James grunted. "Whatever. I'll sign."

Shay looked at him with surprise. "You will?"

"It's like he said." James nodded at the senator. "I have a single magical working for me right now, and one other sort of working for me. I'm never gonna have an army of magicals who can pump me full of magic, so it doesn't even matter. I'll probably only need Modified Forerunner mode if another Vax shows up. Extended Advanced will be enough for everyone else."

James saw no reason to admit to the politician that Whispy's absorption of the Purifier had increased their combined baseline power, endurance, and regeneration even without the Modified Forerunner transformation. The Forerunner was exponentially more powerful in that form than when he first took on the Harriken, although maybe not strong enough to take out an entire city by himself.

No fucking reason for that kind of thing anyway.

Senator Johnston smiled warmly. "Excellent, son. We're all on the same page." He held up his phone. "I've got to go. I'll contact you again in a few days about signing our little agreement. I can cough up a government stipend if you want."

"Nah. I've got plenty of money."

"Then let's say I owe you a few favors." Senator Johnston stood and offered a polite nod to both Shay and James before heading to the front door. He opened it, stepped outside, and closed the door.

Shay gazed at James. "Are you really okay with that?"

"Yeah. I'm semi-retiring anyway after the wedding, so it's not like I'm gonna need to be able to beat down Vax Destroyers. Whispy is adapted to so much shit now it's rare that a level five is much of a problem." James leaned his head back to stare at the ceiling. "And from what Whispy said, the Vax probably aren't gonna come back. All this shit that's been hanging over me my entire life is done. I know everything I need to know now about my past, so I can go on and have a future with you and Alison."

Shay smiled. "It's not too late to uninvite Senator Johnston to the wedding."

James shook his head. "Nah, that's fine."

Shay laughed. "I just thought of something."

"What?"

"You're inviting all the top criminals anyway. Might as well invite politicians."

James snorted. "Yeah, might as well. It's weird, though."

"What?"

"Having only good things to look forward to: the wedding, Alison growing up." James glanced down at his sleeping dog. "I used to be a man with no life whose only real friend was a dog. Now I have a life. It's strange and shit." He shrugged.

"I know the feeling," Shay replied. "Well, I didn't even have a dog. I just ran around killing people and pretending I had a life."

James grinned. "I was the same way."

"One thing, though." Shay shook her finger. "No matter what happens, I don't want you beating up or killing anyone at the wedding. If necessary, you can just write down who pisses you off and kill them after the honeymoon."

"Okay. I promise not to beat up or kill anyone on our wedding day."

Shay stood and stretched. "I'm tired from last night, but I could be persuaded to have a little more fun."

James laughed. "Shouldn't we save some of it for the honeymoon?"

"That's boring. Come on, James." Shay winked. "You just saved the world. Let's spend the next few weeks in bed."

James considered the plan and nodded. "Just put a tray of ribs on the nightstand, and that sounds like heaven."

EPILOGUE

Several months later

The months passed in relative quiet following the fight with the Vax. James didn't even bother taking on the few level fours who came into LA, instead letting his agency handle it. May Wu joining to shore up their magical strength helped with that.

James had spent those months scouting locations for his new barbeque restaurant, but he was having trouble finding a place that fit all his demanding criteria and also didn't threaten to disrupt business for any other close local barbeque venue. He still had another half-dozen promising locations to check out after he returned from his honeymoon.

Just as Senator Johnston predicted, everyone had accepted the government's story at face value. A few people here and there questioned it, but everyone still in the city at the time of the battle hadn't been anywhere near the fight, so all they could claim is that they saw explosions and flashes of light. The government even produced a doctored video showing the alleged artifact, a golden trident, randomly emitting dangerous energy blasts, and the PDA and Oricerans performing a ritual that caused the trident to fire off a final ring of destruction before it disintegrated.

The destruction of Alazi on Oriceran had been successfully attributed to a magical terrorist who had already been sent to the World in Between. Despite what Senator Johnston had told James, the bounty hunter didn't completely understand why the Oricerans had agreed to the cover-up. However, interplanetary politics were too complicated for him to worry about. He suspected there was more *quid pro quo* in the background, the politician wasn't admitting anything.

In the end, it turned out that with enough magic, the government could pull off a near-perfect coverup, even in a city that still held thousands of people. Federal disaster funds had been routed to Los Angeles to help, and additional alumni donations had flooded in to help repair USC.

James wasn't bothered that most people didn't know the truth. He believed everything he had told Senator Johnston about the trouble with his already cumbersome fame. The important thing was that he had done what was needed when the time came, and his future was secure.

Now James stood in a huge bedroom in a mansion on the small island off the coast of California they had rented for the wedding. The damned bedroom was almost the size of his entire first floor. Even though he could afford a home like this, he didn't understand the appeal. Too busy. Too complicated to maintain.

Glad Shay didn't decide to buy the island.

James adjusted his silver cufflinks. He frowned at his dark tuxedo in the full-wall mirror and shook his head. "I can't believe people wear this shit on purpose. I should have just walked out there with Whispy, all armored up and shit. I'm wearing a damned bowtie. Can you believe this?"

Trey laughed. They had discussed the truth about James and his amulet a few weeks after the Battle of LA, as the younger man had taken to calling the incident.

To James' complete lack of surprise, Trey's only response had been to say, "I always knew you were a special motherfucker, but I didn't know you were Moses and Superman rolled up into one."

Among James' groomsmen, Tyler and Mack didn't know the truth. Both were currently out of the room.

"You know what your problem is, big man?" Trey asked, adjusting his own bow tie. "You don't wear enough suits in general. I'm always rocking me some nice threads, so this is just taking shit to the next level."

The Professor fluffed his lapels, not a hint of red in his cheeks. He'd promised not to have a single drop of alcohol until the reception, although he swore he would have *all* the alcohol at that point. James'd had the wedding planner order twice as much beer as they had originally figured, just as a precaution.

"It's good, lad," the Professor suggested, "to dress up every now and again. A man can't always wear jeans and a t-shirt. A certain style and grace can be appealing on a rare occasion."

"I think this tie is choking me out," James complained.

"The great James Brownstone, ladies and gentlemen," Trey responded. "The Harriken couldn't defeat him. The Council couldn't defeat him. Even motherfucking aliens couldn't defeat him, but a tie can." He grinned. "I'll avenge you, brother. I'll fucking kill every bowtie left on this planet."

"Funny." James grunted.

"I know I am."

The door opened to reveal Mack and Tyler.

"That's a *lot* of people," Tyler observed. "Damn, Brownstone, half the freaking underworld bosses in town have come up to me, asking questions about what you think of them. Since when am I your Mob Whisperer?"

James shrugged. "Do what you normally do. Charge their asses."

Tyler rubbed his chin. "You know what? That's a good idea."

Mack closed the door. "I don't think I've ever been to such a huge wedding, even if half the guests are criminals. They *are* better behaved than most of the guests at my sister's last wedding." He nodded at James. "I forgot to tell you. According to the Organized Crime task force and the Gang task force, all crime associated with either major group has dropped to almost nothing over the last couple of weeks. Word is on the street that all the bosses are telling their guys and any gangs they work with to keep everything under control or else, 'Brownstone will end you and everyone you know.'"

"That's not far from the truth," James rumbled. "But I'm glad I could do something to keep things cleaned up for you guys. I feel lazy sometimes, leaving most of it on the agency."

"No, it's good, but I'm personally thinking about retiring soon," Mack admitted. "Real retirement, too, not Maria-going-to-work-for-you-style retirement."

"You could help me with my restaurant, or is that not retirement enough?" James asked.

Mack's eyes widened. "I've been thinking about that, and that sounds like a good idea."

Trey laughed. "All you old men go off and play at running restaurants. Leave the criminals to us young studs."

Mack scoffed. The Professor and Tyler smirked.

Someone knocked lightly on the door.

"Yeah?" James called.

"Mr. Brownstone, we're ready to get started," called Mary Winters. She'd gone from simple wedding planner to Shay's right-hand woman for the entire affair. Coordinating the massive wedding had become a temporary full-time job, complete with multiple assistants.

The Professor smiled. "Are *you* ready, lad? This is a big step."

"Of all the shit I've done, this is the thing that feels the most right," James replied.

"Not exactly a Shakespearean sonnet, but romantic in its own way."

James headed toward the door. "Time to begin the first day of the rest of my life."

James made his way down the red carpet running under the massive shimmering magical field covering the entire area. It wouldn't protect the wedding against a direct missile strike, but the spell did keep the hot July sun from cooking the guests. Steady light breezes blew with the help of air magic throughout the area, keeping everything comfortable for the guests in their elegant suits and dresses.

Guess Mary was right about getting those wedding-support witches. Everyone looks fine. Also glad Shay didn't settle on some of the weirder shit. She seemed really into that flying bouquet idea at first.

The start of the red carpet lay right next to a side entrance to the mansion. The wedding party had taken their positions there, with the exception of Shay, who had decided at the last moment that she believed in the superstition about the bride not seeing the groom before the wedding. Either that, or she just wanted to screw with James a little. He couldn't be sure. He never could with her.

Father McCartney had somehow gotten special dispensation from his bishop for the wedding's location. James didn't question the how and why. He was just glad they wouldn't need to have multiple ceremonies.

Beautiful dulcet music filled the air, provided by a sixteen-piece orchestra. Shay had originally thought about hiring a full orchestra, but James had managed to talk her down by pointing out the logistical difficulties of adding over a hundred more people to the location.

Hundreds of chairs, all filled, surrounded him, the

guests seated without any concern over if they were a guest of the groom or the bride.

The different guests represented all the aspects of his life, positive and negative. He passed a grinning Frank Altieri and several of his goons, and the mobster offered him a polite nod.

Guess Frankie Boy really likes his weddings. I hope he understands there's no bounty hunter tradition that says I have to grant him a favor just because it's my wedding day.

Peyton and his girlfriend sat in the back, also smiling. The bright look on his girlfriend's face suggested she was getting a few ideas of her own about weddings.

Heather sat in her wheelchair at the end of the right front row, holding her son's hand. She'd recently started looking into an experimental spinal cord stimulator—technological, not magical—that might help her walk. James had offered to pay for it, and she was having her first meeting with the doctors in a few weeks.

A few more steps brought James into a cop-heavy crowd. Lieutenant Weber, along with most of the LAPD AET, was there. Other police officers from LA, Vegas, and Detroit filled the rows ahead. Brownstone Agency bounty hunters, along with a few other selected bounty hunters, were scattered throughout the chairs, though most of the OGs sat closer to the front, along with Kathy and most of James' non-field personnel. Even Victoria had come down from Vegas for the wedding.

Charlyce and Nana Garfield sat near the front, Zoe next to them. Senator Johnston and his wife sat close to them, along with several other people from the government. Children from the orphanage and many of the people from the congregation clustered around them as well. He'd never been a man to befriend others from his church, but they all worshipped together. Several of his neighbors, including an ecstatic-looking Mrs. Garth, sat close to them.

James was surprised by some of the people who were invited and showed up. When Shay had asked him for a list of a "few more people to invite," he'd thought of Addie Endo, the high-value courier he'd helped a few times. It wasn't like they were close, but she sat there in a dark-blue dress that contrasted with her pink hair. She grinned merrily and waved at James from the edge of one of the rows.

Dannec was only a few seats down from her. James hadn't been sure whether to invite him, but the elf's help had been critical to James' victories on more than one occasion, including supplying necessary magical items for James' use against the Council and the Drow. Maybe they weren't friends, but it didn't hurt to show the man a little respect by inviting him.

James passed Lily and her friends, the former homeless tunnel rats now all wearing expensive clothes. James was surprised that Lily hadn't been one of the bridesmaids, but Shay explained to him that the girl hadn't been comfortable with the idea. She had adjusted to life as a tomb raider, but she was still finding her feet in normal society.

James held back a smirk as he passed Yev, the Oriceran Consul for Los Angeles. He didn't like the man after the way he had participated, even indirectly, in the Drow legal plots against James and Alison, but since he was inviting the criminal gangs to remind them who he was, it didn't hurt to invite a few high-ranking Oricerans to remind them as well.

The Granite Ghost might be getting married, but he was still the Granite Ghost.

The unpleasantness of James' political enemies was offset by all the pitmasters present, including Mike and Michael from Jessie Rae's. They were helping with the food, too, but he wanted it clear they weren't just caterers. They were honored guests.

James approached the small altar set up at the front of the red carpet near a cliff overlooking the ocean. Seagulls and other ocean birds soared in the distance as a light breeze filled his nostrils with the salty scent of the water.

Father McCartney stood there with a delighted smile on his face. James moved into position and offered a nod to the priest.

The Professor appeared next and joined the groom. Trey escorted Kara up the red carpet, Mack followed with Janelle, and Tyler arrived with Bella. Alison finished the procession by herself. She had volunteered to walk by herself in honor of Shorty.

The bridesmaids all wore lavender gowns that were flattering to the beautiful women and teen. Shay wasn't a believer in her friends having to wear ugly dresses to make her stand out. James wasn't sure whether that was a testament to her loyalty or her complete confidence in her own beauty.

Maria appeared next, a hungry smile on her face as she headed down the carpet, her gaze fixed on Tyler.

Another woman thinking this is a good idea. Sorry, Tyler, you better give up and start planning now.

A huge grin broke across James' face as Thomas padded up the carpet next, the handle of a wicker basket containing the rings on black velvet clutched in his jaws. The crowd produced a chorus of oohs and ahs as the dog carried the rings to the Professor.

I'm glad I convinced Shay to allow this. Way better than a kid doing it.

The Professor knelt, took the basket, and ruffled the dog's ears. Thomas barked once and bounded back down the carpet, just like they had practiced. The crowd laughed.

Thomas disappeared back into the mansion.

The orchestra changed songs, but they didn't play *Here Comes the Bride*. Instead, a jaunty flute-heavy piece followed. It was reminiscent of something James might expect from Greek folk music, but Shay explained it was specifically Cappadocian Greek. She'd gotten the idea after recovering an artifact from the ruins of an old Cappadocian city.

James didn't care. He didn't have any strong preferences when it came to music.

Shay appeared from the mansion clad in a voluminous gown and veil, so elaborate magic had to be involved, much like with her bouquet. It might not be flying, but it was still obviously the product of enchantment.

The bride clutched the glowing flowers, each cycling through different colors. She made her way down the aisle by herself. Her past was gone, dead along with her past identity and any connection to her worthless parents. The only thing important now was her future.

The music stopped as Shay stepped up to the priest and James. She pulled back her veil and smiled at James.

Father McCartney brought his hand to his mouth and coughed, then began, "Dearly beloved, we are gathered here today in the sight of friends, family, and God, to witness the joining of James Brownstone and Shay Carson in holy matrimony."

James stared into Shay's dark eyes, his priest's words growing distant and indistinct. As much as he respected Father McCartney, he didn't need pretty words to understand how he felt. He loved Shay, and she completed him. That was enough.

He managed the appropriate nods and verbal agreements as the priest launched into a series of questions. Something about love. Something about honoring the church.

Wait. I need to pay attention. The vows are coming.

The Professor handed James and Shay rings.

"Please repeat after me," Father McCartney intoned. "I, James Brownstone, take you, Shay Carson, for my lawful wife, to have and to hold from this day forward, for better, for worse, for richer, for poorer, in sickness and in health, until death us do part."

James repeated the vows as he slipped the wedding ring over Shay's finger. The jeweler he'd hired had been shocked by his desire to cut down a "perfectly good diamond." James had it checked to ensure it wasn't magical, but in the end, the *lele* had given him a large and expensive but mundane gemstone.

"And you, Shay," Father McCartney insisted.

"I, Shay Carson, take you, James Brownstone, for my lawful husband, to have and to hold from this day forward, for better, for worse, for richer, for poorer, in sickness and in health, until death us do part."

Shay slipped James' wedding band over his finger.

"Then by the power invested me by the Church and the state of California, I now pronounce you man and wife," Father McCartney announced, beaming with happiness.

A raucous cheer rose from the army of wedding guests. Among others, Nana Garfield clapped and teared up.

"You may now kiss the bride," Father McCartney added.

James pulled Shay against him and attacked her mouth with all the hunger he felt.

James couldn't help but stare at his new wife. They sat together at a table, along with the Professor, Maria, Tyler, Alison, and Father McCartney. A maze of white-linen-covered wooden tables filled the vast lawn in front of the mansion, expensive magic still protecting the guests. Light orbs surrounded the tables and pushed back the early evening darkness.

The time since the vows had passed in a blur of smiles, backslaps, handshakes, and congratulations. They were supposed to be eating now, but even though the most glorious tray of ribs slathered in God Sauce sat in front of James, he didn't care about barbeque. It turned out there were a few things he cared more about than grilled and sauced meat.

The only person with a wider grin at the table was Alison, who kept giggling. "Now you can't complain about me calling you mom, Mom."

Shay laughed. "You got me there. Just so you know, I'm also going to do the formal paperwork to adopt you. I don't just want to be your stepmother. I want to be your mother."

Alison threw her arms around Shay's neck and hugged her tightly.

Warmth spread through James. A few years prior he had met Alison by chance when she returned his dog. He had never expected to grow to love her as a daughter, nor the strong-willed but caustic woman who had become his wife.

Thank you, God, for all that you've given me. I know I've not always been the best man, but I've tried my best.

Senator Johnston made his way up to the table. "Sorry to bother you while you're eating, son, but I figured it was a good time for my gift."

"Gift?" James blinked a few times. "No one needed to bring any gifts. We said that in the invitations."

The old man laughed. "I'm too old-fashioned. There's no way I'm going to come to a wedding without a gift. Besides, I already cleared it with your bride."

James looked at Shay, and she smiled at him and shrugged. "I know you said you didn't care about gifts, but I asked a couple of the guests to kick in on the entertainment."

Senator Johnston patted James on the shoulder. "Congratulations again, son. You'll enjoy being married. I know I have, and I've been married longer than you've been alive." He headed back to his table.

A few elves in powder-blue leisure suits walked toward a portable stage set up a few yards away from

James' and Shay's table. A lumbering Kilomea joined them.

"Who are they?" James rumbled.

"Oriceran cover band," Shay announced.

"Seriously?"

A rumble sounded in the distance, and James frowned and looked around. There wasn't a cloud in the sky, so he didn't understand how there could be a storm.

If some wizard fucks up my wedding, I'll go Modified Forerunner on his ass.

Shay grinned. "Yep. Well, don't know if they count as a band since they use magic instead of instruments, but same idea. Needed a little fun for the reception. They have some spells to prep while the initial entertainment happens." She nodded at the Professor.

The best man stood, already red-faced from the four beers he'd pounded. He tugged slightly on his bowtie, and it glowed. "Ladies and gentleman," he began, his voice coming from all around.

Magic megaphone bowtie? Now I've seen everything.

"The new Mrs. Carson-Brownstone turned down my idea for a dirty limerick contest in the middle of the wedding," the Professor explained with a grin. "Absolutely no sense of humor, but before I bore you with a speech about the greatness of the new couple, there are several different people who wanted to pay their respects."

The rumble built and everyone looked around, a few nervously. The Professor's smile grew only wider, as did the one on Senator Johnston, who stood nearby.

What did you plan?

"Everyone knows how much bounty work James has

performed," the Professor observed. "But that often conceals how he's helped defend his country. Some of the targets he's taken down, well, some of you wouldn't be able to sleep at night if you knew what had been out there. The military has worked side by side with the good lad, and with the help of Senator Johnston, the United States Air Force has a little demonstration for us to pay him back for all that."

The rumble became a roar as six fighter planes approached in rapid formation. State-of-the-art F-55s broke apart and released trails of red, white, and blue smoke, their adjustable vector thrust nozzles allowing them to bank and turn so abruptly it almost seemed like magic.

An air show at my wedding? Shit. Nice.

While that was a miracle of technology, James suspected the diffuse glow surrounding the planes and making them so visible at night was the product of actual magic—not that he was going to complain.

James might not have liked flying, but he didn't mind watching it. He grinned at Shay as one of the fighters barrel-rolled.

Fifteen minutes later, the fighters zoomed away to the cheering and applause of the wedding guests.

The Professor rose again. "Consul Yev has arranged a little something as well."

The Light Elf rose and bowed, then raised his hands and opened his mouth. The melodious chords of his native speech filled the air, and several of the magical guests exchanged curious looks.

At least no one looks scared.

Multiple portals opened high above the guests, and dozens of pulsating orbs slowly floated out.

James narrowed his eyes, not sure what was going on. He spared a glance at Shay, and she looked up with a smile on her face.

Okay, so it's not some sort of ambush.

James patted his chest, comforted by the weight of Whispy beneath his shirt. He didn't want to have to go all Vax at his wedding.

The orbs spun and flung out shimmering sparks at high speed. The glowing sparks separated into strings of light, and soon the entire sky was painted in luminous strings. A few seconds later, one of them exploded in a colorful ring. Then another, and another.

The flames and sparks formed different shapes: an elf dancing, a bird flying, a waterfall. The living explosions continued decorating the sky, to the cheering delight of the crowd.

Sometimes the simplest pleasures were the best.

James furrowed his brow at the thought.

Wait. I've gotten a military air show, and now magical fireworks. That shit isn't simple.

James held Shay in his arms as they swayed to the music for the first dance of the reception. Several other couples had already joined them. The elves sang in their native language, the melodies overlapping and communicating love and respect, or maybe they were just saying how much Earth sucked and making it sound nice to human ears. James didn't care either way.

"How's the wedding?" Shay asked. "You didn't pay much attention when we were planning it, so I didn't know how much it might surprise you."

"Fucking complicated," James replied.

Shay laughed. "It's only one day in your entire life." She leaned forward to whisper, "I tried to get Johnston to let us have it on the vimana, but apparently that's another thing half the fucking world has to sign off on before they allow anyone to use it."

James grunted. "Floating castle-islands are worse than planes."

"I guess I'm lucky he told me no, then." Shay laid her head on his shoulder. "Am I going to be enough for you?"

"Why wouldn't you be?"

Shay smiled. "Because I'm the world's sexiest and smartest human, but I'm just a human, in the end."

"No, you're not 'just' anything. You're my wife, which means you're the most important woman in the world."

Shay's breath caught, and her cheeks reddened. "Why, Mr. Brownstone, you can actually pull off a few romantic words without involving dirty limericks."

"On occasion."

The slow song stopped, and the music changed. It took James' brain a few seconds to catch up to the fact the band was now singing what sounded like a country song, with the Kilomea growling out vocals in his native language— which was far less aesthetically pleasing than the Light

Elves' melodies. Something sounded very familiar about the song.

James blinked. "What are they singing?"

Shay laughed. "I couldn't resist. I talked to Smite-Williams about it after I heard it on an oldies station the other day."

"What song, though?"

Shay gestured toward the band. "It's a Kilomea language cover of Billy Ray Cyrus' *Achy Breaky Heart*."

"Huh," James replied, and shook his head. "What a world."

He surveyed the happy, dancing crowd with a smile on his face. His life hadn't been free from pain and loss—the empty spot and chair for Shorty was a poignant reminder of that—but in the last several years, he had found something beyond mere existence.

Life. Love. Family. Friendship.

The Granite Gargoyle now had a family. He now had a true future. James couldn't help the stupid grin taking over his face.

"What are you thinking?" Shay asked.

"Just about how lucky I am. I love you, Shay."

"I love you, too, James."

Eight years later

James entered his house and closed the door behind him.

Shay sat on the couch, her hands folded in her lap. She wore the same look on her face she always had whenever she was waiting for him with important news.

Uh-oh. Here comes the ambush.

James slipped off his coat and put it in the closet. "Alison didn't get a new boyfriend, did she? The one she has now is okay. He's got some balls, and I can respect it. And he's not a vegetarian."

Shay's face twitched. "It's good that you like him because they're moving in together."

"What?" James growled. "Wait one damned moment. It's one thing for him to date her, but moving in together? I didn't agree to that."

Shay rolled her eyes. "She's a grown woman, James. She doesn't need your permission to move in with her boyfriend."

"He does to move in with her." James stomped over to his recliner. "I don't like how fast this relationship is progressing."

"You know what your problem is? You still see Alison as—"

"That little girl who brought you your dog," James finished for her, and shrugged. "I know. You tell me that all the time." He nodded to his sleeping dog beside the couch. "So often that Thomas is probably beginning to think it's another name for him."

"And I'm gonna keep telling you." Shay let out a frustrated laugh. "And I shouldn't have to tell a man who doesn't forget things the same thing over and over, don't you think?"

"I'm just saying it would be nice if she could have given me a little warning."

"I'm interested in what would have happened if you had raised her from birth," Shay replied, a coy smile appearing.

"Huh? What do you mean?"

Shay shrugged. "Just, if you had to deal with a kid from birth, how would things be different?"

"Not like it's gonna happen, so why worry about it?" James cracked his knuckles, wondering if he should travel up to Seattle and have another conversation with Alison's boyfriend. Or kick him through a wall.

I turn my back for one second, and the guy's moving in.

Shay cleared her throat. "Say, have you ever bitched to Whispy about not being able to have a kid?"

James stared at Shay. "Huh. It's not like I have family talks with him the few times a year I use him. We get down to business. He mostly bitches about the fact that I don't have enough new adaptations for him, but he's still the same Whispy Doom. It's not like he cares about family or love, and I'm certainly not gonna discuss my sex life with some biomechanical symbiont. Why?"

"Oh, it's just that he's still tinkering with you." Shay rubbed the back of her neck. "You've told me that. He's always tweaking something here or there. I get that you don't wear him as much anymore, but that means he could make a big change and you might not know it for months."

James nodded. "Sure, but he always tells me what he's going to do before he changes anything."

"But you've also told me that sometimes there can be unexpected side effects."

Why does she look so nervous?

"Yeah," James rumbled. "Changing me to be more human rather than Vax means he's not always sure about what shit's gonna happen, but there's been nothing too bad, other than that…thing in Bali, but we're not gonna talk about that."

Shay licked her lips. "James, I'm pregnant."

"Yeah, that's…" James shot out of the chair. "What? *What?*"

"I'm pregnant." Shay shrugged. "It's confirmed. You're going to be a father."

James stared at Shay, his mouth agape.

"Woah," James managed.

Shay walked over and kissed him on the cheek. "I'll get to see how Daddy Brownstone operates when he doesn't start with a teenager. This ought to be interesting."

"Woah," James repeated.

Shay grinned. "You seem a little overwhelmed. Maybe you should go on one of your barbeque road trips and let it sink in." She cupped her stomach. "Because in a few short months, we'll be welcoming a new Brownstone."

AUTHOR NOTES - MICHAEL ANDERLE
AND RVINGPSYCHIC

APRIL 18, 2019

THANK YOU for not only reading this story but these *Author Notes* as well.

(I think I've been good with always opening with "thank you." If not, I need to edit the other *Author Notes*!)

Thank you ALL for supporting this amazing series with these characters I love. When I was working with a partner on figuring out the plotline, it became obvious that I could only take the series so far. I had to stop it before it ran on too long.

Plus, what are you going to do when you've kicked the Vax's asses?

Well, I have some bad news —and some good news.

This is the end of Brownstone...and yet, *NOT* the end.

I'm planning on something loosely (very loosely) based on the buddy films of a long time ago, where Brownstone goes on the road to find BBQ and stuff happens. Stuff that requires him to use a sufficient amount of force to save a locality...and BBQ.

These stories will arrive about every three months, so please be on the lookout!

Just a note—I hope we are about...eighteen days?? Or so (I am going to need to look at a calendar) from Bethany Anne coming out. Just saying, it should be in the next few weeks.

New artwork is up on the Facebook Page for Bethany Anne, so come check it out, and if you see the following fan who responding to my request to "tell me a bit about you," say hi!

Q & A

I would like to introduce LMBPN reading fan RVing-Psychic, who wrote these notes while in Jacksonville, Florida (If I have comments, they are at the end of their responses.)

M: About how many books do you read a year, or total in your lifetime?

R: 300-500 a year (Mike: Ok, kicks my ass completely. That's like 25 to 40+ a month. Not in my best month did I read that many.)

M: Name your favorite LMBPN Series or Character(s) and what you like about them.

R: Bethany Anne the original series, and Federation Witch is also high up on the list. (Mike: Awesome! I'm happy that I was able to create a series where I didn't kill off the parents and yet fans got into the character.)

M: If you made up an LMBPN Character, what three attributes would you use? (For Example, Bethany Anne is about Justice, Family (including friends), and Coca Cola. Brownstone is Keeping it Simple, Respect, and BBQ)

R: Strength, Justice, and love of animals (Mike – I might have to handle the animals thing a bit different than how I started Brownstone – Although he does love his dog(s).)

M: Tell us a few short sentences about yourself and your reading hobby (When did you start reading, why, how much do you read, and preferred genre's, etc. (as ideas)):

R: I started when I was about 4 and have never stopped. I actually love fantasy, SciFi, and Paranormal, but I will read anything that grabs my attention, including non-fiction.

I love falling into a story and being a part of it.

M: You can have my <what?> before you can have my reading time.

R: Anything! Reading is super important. (Mike: Yeah, I feel you, but I might have a couple of things someone can't have before reading. Not that any come to mind at the moment.)

M: Place you have loved to read the most in your life —best memory(s) (mine was as a teenager at my grandparents' house under the feather bed on cold days.)

R: Laying on a blanket on a warm day under a tree. (Mike: I've done this one time at my house in Katy – It had the PERFECT ring for my head to rest… I fell asleep.)

AROUND THE WORLD IN 80 DAYS

One of the interesting (at least to me) aspects of my life is the ability to work from anywhere and at any time. In the future, I hope to re-read my own *Author Notes* and remember my life as a diary entry.

WHERE AM I?

Cabin in the Sky (™) Las Vegas, Nevada

So, I'm at my desk typing this for tomorrow's release, having just had a full day of conference calls (some for stories, some for business operations) and having read the beats for the new *Animus* book Joshua is writing and a scene from Elaine Bateman's upcoming book.

Tomorrow, I get to sit in on a consulting meeting where an individual from San Diego is going to suggest ways to do better selling paperbacks. I'm looking forward to the discussions, and I hope they have some new info we can use!

Selling paperbacks is a tough business, and (so far) there has been very little money in it for us.

FAN PRICING

$0.99 Saturdays (new LMBPN stuff) and $0.99 Wednesday (both LMBPN books and friends of LMBPN books.) Get great stuff from us and others at tantalizing prices.

Go ahead. I bet you can't read just one.

Sign up here: http://lmbpn.com/email/.

HOW TO MARKET FOR BOOKS YOU LOVE

Review them so others have your thoughts, and tell friends and the dogs of your enemies (because who wants to talk to enemies?)... *Enough said ;-)*

Ad Aeternitatem,
Michael Anderle

CONNECT WITH MICHAEL ANDERLE

Michael Anderle Social
   Website:
   http://www.lmbpn.com

Email List:
   http://lmbpn.com/email/

Facebook Here:
   https://www.facebook.com/OriceranUniverse/
   https://www.
facebook.com/TheKurtherianGambitBooks/